Martha's Fun Summer
Written by: Bekah O'Brien
Illustrated by: Bethany O'Brien

This book is dedicated to Jesus, my best Friend and Savior, and to Shaynie, my writing mentor and wonderful sister in Christ.

2 Corinthians 2:14
"Now thanks be unto God, which always causeth us to triumph in Christ, and maketh manifest the savour of his knowledge by us in every place."

I hope you enjoy my book!

The Knight Family

Peter Knight (Dad)
Rosemary Knight (Mom)
Children:
Martha, (age 12)
Thomas, (age 10)
Twins: James, (age 8)
Anna, (age 8)
Lydia, (age 5)
Sarah, (age 3)
Elizabeth, (age 1)

Chapters

Chapter 1
Plans Over Breakfast

It was July 1, 1930, and summer was officially underway. Twelve-year-old Martha Knight woke to the delicious aroma that was wafting into her room. She knew that her mom was making breakfast. *Hmm, it smells like pancakes! I better get up and get dressed.* Martha got up and dressed in her day dress, put her work apron on, braided her light brown hair, washed her face, and made her bed. She then went downstairs and out the back door, first giving her Mom a kiss. "See you at breakfast, Martha." At five feet, six inches tall, Rosemary Knight had blonde hair with sparkling blue eyes. She is the mother of six children and wife to her husband, Peter.

Once Martha got to the barn, she saw her brothers, ten-year-old Thomas milking the cow and eight-year old James raking out the stalls. Martha got some oats for the horses and put them in the trough. "Hey, James, what have you got planned for this lovely Saturday afternoon?" asked Martha.

"Well, I think I'd like to do some fishing this afternoon. Would you like to come along?" James asked with a smile, already knowing what her answer would be.

"Not this time. Besides, I really don't like cleaning the fish. You might ask Anna though."

"You know, you'll have to clean them for your future husband one day," teased James. While Thomas was quiet, kind and thoughtful, James was fun-loving and sometimes liked to joke around with his sister.

Martha hid her smile before she turned around. "Let's not go putting the cart before the horse. I'll cross that bridge when I come to it," she answered as she hurried to the chicken coop before James could say anything else.

About twenty minutes later, everyone gathered around the table and Dad bowed his head with the others following his lead.

"Dear Father in Heaven, thank You for this food that You have provided for us. Thank You for the hands that prepared it. Amen."

Everyone dug into the meal and thanked Mom for it; then Thomas asked, "Dad, what's in store for our summer?"

"Well," Dad began, "first of all, your Mom and I are extremely proud of you children for helping around the farm. You all are such a blessing. We have been thinking and talking about it and at the end of August, we are going to hold a party with a dance at our place and--"

"What's the date, Dad?" Martha interrupted.

"Whoa! Let me finish. We will have a lot of work ahead of us, cleaning and getting the garden ready before we can really dig into this upcoming event. We have considered August 24th for a good date, but that's not all. We are also going to renew our vows at the party!"

"What's 'new' your vows mean, Daddy?" asked three-year-old Sarah.

"Well, it's kind of like a wedding, but we are just going to say our vows to each other again. We're going to remind everyone how much we love each other. Does that make sense?" asked Dad.

"Yes, Daddy, it does n-now," said Sarah, pronouncing her words carefully.

"Well, what does everybody think about this plan?" Mom smiled at everyone as she reached for the plate of pancakes.

"YES! We love it. We want you and Dad to renew your vows," said all the children in unison, except for baby Elizabeth, who was too little to say anything except 'mama' and 'da-da'.

"Anna, would you please take Sarah to get her face washed?" asked Mom after breakfast was finished and Martha and Sarah began the process of kitchen clean-up.

"Sure, Mom," said Anna, who was eight, and James's twin sister.

After the dishes were done and three-year-old Sarah had had her face washed by her big sister, everyone crowded into the living room to have morning family devotions. "Today," started Dad, "we are going to be reading in Philippians 4:13. Rosemary, would you read that to us please?" Dad smiled at Mom.

"Sure," Mom returned. *"I can do all things through Christ which strengtheneth me."*

"Let's think on this for a moment. Paul is trying to tell us something here. We need to rely on God's strength and ability to help us rather than our own strength. Sometimes it is hard to rely on God when we're so puffed up with pride about what we can do. But it's necessary to humble ourselves that we can do ALL things through CHRIST who strengthens me. Does anyone have questions?" Dad paused, and there were no questions so he continued, "Well, Rosemary, would you lead us in the 'Solid Rock' please?"

"I'd love to!" Mom started in her clean, crisp voice and the others followed her lead.

Chapter 2
Garden

"Anna! Lydia!" Martha called. "Are you ready to go work in the garden?" Sarah was playing in the living room with some puzzles and Elizabeth was playing with some blocks in her high chair.

"Yes, we're coming," answered Anna for both of them. A minute later, Anna came from their room and Lydia followed with something that looked like a dead mouse. "Lydia, what do you have?" questioned Martha.

"A mouse," Lydia replied matter-of-factly.

"Ah! Mom, Lydia has a dead mouse by the tail!" Martha yelled from the front porch. If there was one thing that Martha didn't like, it was mice. Mom came hurrying from the kitchen where she had been mopping. She carried a brown paper bag she had saved from one of her trips to the market.

"Here, put him in this," she offered.

"Thanks, Mom." Martha worked at getting the thing into the bag without touching it.

"Lydia, you need to go and wash your hands. Where did you find that mouse?" questioned Mom.

"Under the bed," Lydia replied, wondering what the fuss was about.

"Okay, I'll have your Dad look for a mouse hole in your room when he and the boys come home from the field."

While Lydia washed her hands in the sink in the upstairs bath, Anna and Martha went to the barn for the gardening tools before heading out toward the garden behind the house. When they got there, Lydia was waiting for them with her little doll in hand.

"Lydia, you shouldn't take Polly to work in the garden. Just lean her on that tree over there. I think she'll be okay," Anna directed.

"Okay, Anna," said Lydia, skipping over to the tree.

Martha and Anna started pulling the weeds and when Lydia came back she went to fill the water bucket. When she returned, she set the bucket on the ground. When Martha reached to take the pail, it felt light, so she looked inside. "Oh Lydia you-" she stopped mid-sentence, thinking; *she didn't mean to spill half the bucket.*

Martha poured the bit of water on one of the plants and held out her hand. "Lydia, would you like to come with me to get some more water?"

"Sure, Martha," Lydia smiled at her big sister and grabbed her hand.

"Good, let's go then." They walked to the pump and Lydia pumped the water. When the bucket was full, Martha helped carry it back to the garden.

About an hour and a half later, Martha looked up to the sun and guessed it was about 11:30. "That's enough for today. Lydia, why don't you go get your doll while Anna and I put the gardening tools away?"

"Okay, Martha," replied Lydia.

Lydia went to get her doll, but when she saw it, it was a pitiful sight. Polly's button eyes were stripped out, one of her hands was torn, and her yarn hair was all knotty. The Knight's dog, Nellie, sat beside it, a look of shame on her face.

"NELLIE!" Lydia yelled and started to cry. She picked up the doll and ran toward Martha and Anna who were coming out of the barn. When they saw her, they hurried toward her and met her halfway.

"Nellie chewed up Polly," wailed Lydia as a big tear ran down her cheek.

"Oh, Lydia, I'm so sorry," Anna said lovingly, feeling guilty that she'd told Lydia to put her doll on the ground. "I'm so sorry I told you to put Polly under the tree where Nellie could get it. Do you

12

forgive me?"

"Y-yes," Lydia hiccupped, as her crying stopped.

"May I see the doll for a minute?" asked Martha.

"Yes."

Martha took the doll in her hands and examined it. "I think I can fix her, Lydia. With a little thread and a needle, your doll will be good as new. I'll try to fix her tonight."

Lydia grinned up at Martha, her tears already dried. "Thank you, Martha." Lydia hugged Martha around the waist where she could reach.

"You're welcome. May I keep your doll until she's fixed, please?"

"Sure. I don't mind, so long as you can fix Polly."

"Thanks." Martha gave her little sister a big hug.

After lunch, it was baking time. Every month they liked to bake a few pies, whether sweet or savory, from the produce of their garden and berries they had canned the year before.

Mom, Martha, and Anna prepared for baking by washing their hands and putting on their aprons. Martha and Anna both started rolling out the dough that Mom had already made earlier in the day, while Mom started making the breads. About twenty minutes later Martha asked, "Anna, could you finish the dough by yourself? There are just about four more rolls you need to roll out. I need to start peeling and cutting the apples and peaches and sprinkling them with cinnamon and lemon juice."

"Sure, Martha, you go right ahead," replied Anna, happy that her older sister depended on her.

"Thanks, Anna," smiled Martha, "Mom, where did you put the lemon juice when you squeezed it from the lemons yesterday?"

"It's in the icebox," Mom replied, her hands messy with flour.

"Thanks." Martha rushed to the icebox in the corner of the kitchen.

"You're welcome," Mom returned cheerfully.

When Martha came back with the lemon juice, Anna had already started peeling the peaches. "I had trouble finding the lemon juice. Sorry it took me so long."

"That's all right, Sis," replied Anna. "I got you

a knife and the basket of apples so you can start right away."

"Thanks Anna, you're a great sister!" Martha gave her sister the warmest smile.

After supper, the Knight family had their evening devotions, and then everyone had free time.

Martha got a needle, thread and yarn to repair Lydia's doll. Lydia stood beside her, watching each stitch Martha made. Thomas and James were playing a game of checkers, Anna worked on her needle point, Dad and Mom talked with baby Elizabeth in Mom's lap, and Sarah was sitting at Dad's knee, looking at a picture book.

There was a knock at the door and Dad got up from his chair to answer it. Martha stopped sewing for a moment and strained her neck to see who it was, but it was too dark to see. So Martha decided to be content, and went back to repairing the doll. She had finished the hair and was just about to start sewing the second little button eye on when the Poltor family stepped in.

"Rosemary, would you please get the Poltors some refreshments? I'm afraid their wagon broke down as they were coming home from town." Dad explained.

"I'd be happy to," replied Mom.

"Mom, why don't you and Mrs. Poltor talk for a bit? I'll get the milk and cookies and bring them in here," Martha offered.

"That would be very nice of you. Thank you, Martha," Mom beamed.

"You're welcome." Martha looked at Dad to see his nod of approval. "Lydia, do you mind if I finish your doll tomorrow night?"

"No, I don't mind, Martha," Lydia answered sweetly.

"Thanks, Lydia. I really appreciate it." Martha put the doll on the side table beside the chair. Anna started for the kitchen and Martha motioned for the Poltor's youngest daughter, thirteen-year-old Mary, to follow them.

Once the girls got to the kitchen Mary let out an excited burst of giggles.

"What are you giggling about?" Martha eyed her friend curiously.

"Guess what?" started Mary mysteriously.

"What?" Martha echoed as she moved about the kitchen.

"Samuel is getting married in January!" Samuel was the eldest Poltor, and eighteen years old.

"He is? Oh how wonderful!" Martha smiled dreamily as she placed cookies on a plate. "Anna, can you get the milk, please?"

Anna nodded and took the milk from the icebox.

Mary smiled and twirled around. "Yes, I can't wait to be a sister-in-law, and hopefully an aunt in a few years!"

"That will be SO exciting! I'm so happy for you!" Martha exclaimed.

"Me, too!" Anna piped up.

"Please don't tell anybody at church tomorrow. We'll announce it tomorrow after the sermon, but since we're here, my family decided to tell your folks and my parents allowed me to tell you two. Please don't think us rude to not tell your little sisters; we just don't want them to accidentally tell. Mother and Father will let Thomas and James know, as well. Oh, I'm just SO excited!" Mary had to be careful not to slosh the milk out of the cups she carried she was so thrilled.

"That's okay; I know you have no intention of being rude."

"Thanks, Martha. I knew you would

understand," replied Mary.

Even from the family room, the families couldn't help overhearing Anna, Mary and Martha's excitement.

"From the sound of it, Mary already told the girls about me." Samuel grinned with pleasure.

"We are so very happy for you! Who's the girl?" Mom smiled widely.

"I don't think you know her, but her name is Grace Under. I've been courting her for about six months. She lives about five miles from here."

"That's wonderful, Samuel. I hope we will be invited to the wedding," said Dad with a twinkle in his eye.

"Oh, of course," assured Samuel. "You're the first to know, so please don't tell anyone at church tomorrow. We will announce it after the service."

"Oh, okay, we won't," Dad assured.

"Will you still be staying here in Helena, Montana?" James asked as he and Thomas joined the conversation.

"Yes, I think so. We plan to build near my parents. We have several acres of land right next door, which will be nice and...."

Meanwhile Anna, Martha and Mary, who had served the milk and cookies several minutes before, were sitting on the floor munching on some when Sarah starting whining. "I wunnt o-nn-e."

"Can you say please?"

"P-plee-se?" said Sarah.

"Yes, you may." Martha smiled and split her cookie with her.

"I wish I had a lot of brothers and sisters like you!" Mary said a bit wistfully.

"Yes, it is nice having a lot of siblings, but they can be a lot of work sometimes." Martha brushed the crumbs from Sarah's dress as she gave her friend a pointed look.

"Yes, but I still think it would be fun," Mary insisted.

"Yes, it is ... yes, they are." Martha looked at her friend, then around at her siblings, realizing how blessed she really was to have a lot of brothers and sisters.

Mary took Sarah on her lap while she finished her cookie and the girls continued talking, but Martha kept that previous conversation in her mind for a long time.

About an hour later, after Dad helped Mr. Poltor fix their wagon, the families said goodbye and the Poltors left.

Chapter 3
Sunday

The next morning, Martha woke up, stretched, and yawned. *Today is Sunday. I wonder what we have planned for the day?* She got out of bed and got dressed.

She went outside to milk the cows and feed the chickens. Then she went upstairs to dress Elizabeth and Sarah. She gently woke dark-haired, blue-eyed Elizabeth, undressed her, changed her diaper and put her in her best dress. She then woke Sarah and helped her dress, held their hands and went down to breakfast.

After the prayer was said and everybody started eating Martha asked, "Dad, what are we going to do today?"

"Well," started Dad, "after we get home from church -- your mother and I want to chat a bit after the service -- I need to do some barn chores after lunch. I think we will make some of the party's to-do list. As a treat, I think we will have a picnic and we will invite Pastor Michael and Janelle Share to come and join us, if they have no other engagements. What do you think, children?" asked Dad.

"That sounds wonderful," Martha replied, and the others added their own excited remarks. Even little Elizabeth clapped her hands in glee.

After breakfast Mom asked, "Martha, while I freshen myself up for church, would you and Sarah clear the table?"

"Yes, ma'am, we'd be happy to!" Martha answered, looking at Sarah who nodded, happy to be around her big sister.

Mom left the table with Elizabeth on her hip to have Elizabeth's face washed thoroughly. Dad went to freshen himself as well and to hitch up the horses. Who knew where the boys had gone, and Lydia and Anna went to collect the Bibles.

Sarah asked, "Marta, wat te pardy goin' to be ike?"

"Well, I suppose us children will help the guests get seated and comfortable and Mom and Dad will renew their vows. Then we will probably have a buffet style supper and then anyone who wants to can dance! It's going to be a really fun time and your friends Kathy and Carolyn will be coming too!"

"'What's a 'buff-ay?'" asked Sarah.

"Well, a buffet is usually a table filled with all sorts of foods, even desserts," answered Martha. She tickled Sarah on her nose and she giggled and jumped back, giving her blonde hair a jounce and her delicate blue eyes twinkled.

"I can't wait!" exclaimed Sarah, drying the last dish.

"Well, let's go and brush our teeth and get in the wagon," suggested Martha.

"'Marta,'" started Sarah, "will you teach me how to dance?"

"Certainly, we'll start tomorrow," replied Martha.

After the service ended, Martha went to find her friends Mary Poltor, Polly McShire and Cathryn and Rose Williams.

She found Polly and Rose first. "Hi Polly, hi Rose, how are you doing?" asked Martha.

"We're fine, how about you?" replied Rose sweetly.

Martha smiled back. "I'm fine. Guess what?" she asked in a hushed tone.

"What?" asked both girls, clearly excited.

"My parents are going to renew their vows at a party!" replied Martha, just as excitedly.

"Oh, such fun, you'll invite us won't you?" asked Polly.

"Oh yes, of course!" Martha grabbed their hands, pulling her friends to go stand outside to talk.

After the Knights got home, Martha went up to her room to change from her best dress to her day dress, then came downstairs to help with lunch.

"How were Rose and Polly today?" asked Mom.

"They were fine. I told them about the party," Martha told her.

"Were they excited?" questioned Mom.

"Oh yes, very excited," replied Martha.

"Will you take these sandwiches to the table and get drinks for everyone please?" asked Mom kindly.

"Sure, Mom," Martha went to carry out her tasks.

About five minutes later everyone sat down to lunch in their everyday clothes. After Dad blessed the food, everybody started eating.

Dad turned to his eldest daughter, "Martha, while the boys are out with me, your Mom wants to take a short nap with Elizabeth, so that means you will need to take care of Anna, Lydia, and Sarah."

"Can we go down to the creek?" asked Martha.

"No, I'll need you to stay here where you can be near Elizabeth if she wakes up early."

"Yes, Dad, may we sit out on the porch where maybe a nice cool breeze will hit us?" asked Martha.

"Yes, you may. I think that would be fine," replied Dad.

"Have Michael and Janelle agreed to join our picnic?" asked Mom.

"Yes, they said they would arrive at some time around five o'clock," replied Dad.

"Oh good, they are always nice to be around. I can't wait to chat with Janelle," said Mom excitedly. Martha smiled at her mother, happy just because her mom was.

"Okay, I think everyone is done with their lunch. We will have a party meeting in about two hours. It is about one o'clock now so we should meet here at three o'clock," said Dad.

Everyone scattered to his or her own assignments. Martha laid baby Elizabeth down for her afternoon nap and then went out on the porch where her sisters were already sitting on the steps playing hand games.

Martha decided to sit on a porch chair and read. She got her book and sat on the chair and read until she heard some crying. Anna ran to her. "I s-scraped m-my kn-nee!"

"Oh, let's look at it," said Martha kindly as Lydia and Sarah looked on in sad fascination.

Anna showed her hurt knee. "What are we going to do?"

"Well, we need to clean it. Stay here for a moment. I'll be right back." Martha grabbed Lydia's and Sarah's hands and took them to the kitchen. She quickly gathered some books for them to look at. "I need to fix up Anna's knee, so you stay right here. I'll be back in about ten minutes."

Martha went back to Anna and took her to the girls' room and quietly, so as not to wake sleeping Elizabeth, Martha took a basin and filled it with water and took a rag and wet it and started cleaning it. When Anna winced and made a sobbing noise, Martha gave her a stern look and whispered roughly, "Anna, you're going to have to keep from crying."

Anna, trying not to cry, nodded her head. When Martha noticed her tears, she felt the

Holy Spirit convict her, saying: *You don't need to get frustrated at her. Pain is pain, no matter how old you are. What would Jesus do?* Martha immediately regretted talking to her sister in that way and whispered, "I'm sorry. It's not your fault. Will you forgive me for whispering rudely and for the mean face I made?"

Anna whispered, "Yes, of course," and smiled, which made Martha feel ten times better.

About an hour later, everyone crowded into the kitchen and sat down, waiting for the meeting to begin. Finally, Dad raised his hand and the whole family quieted down.

"We are here to discuss the party we are going to be holding in late August. Mom and I have written a list for each of you to get done by August 24th." Dad handed out the lists. Everybody opened theirs to look at their assignments until Dad said, "I would like you not to read your lists now so we can move on with the meeting."

Everyone laid down their lists and continued listening to Dad.

After the meeting Martha went to put her list on the desk in the girls' room. Looking at it on the way, she read:

1. Make invitations for guests
2. Go grocery shopping
3. Clean and prepare yard
4. Make placement cards

"Okay, this won't be too hard. I can send out the invitations next week. I'll start on cleaning the yard tomorrow and-"

"Martha, would you read me my list?" asked Lydia, interrupting her older sister. "I can't make it all out."

"Sure Lydia, I'd be happy to!" agreed Martha, pleasantly. Anna and Lydia had a combined list to work on together.

Anna's and Lydia's list read:

1. Blow up balloons
2. Draw banners
3. Fold tablecloths
4. Clean picnic tables

"Thanks, Sis!" replied Lydia.

"You are welcome," replied Martha.

"Martha! Would you please answer the door? It's probably our guests."

"Yes ma'am," replied Martha. She was glad

Pastor and Mrs. Share had agreed to have a picnic with them. Martha opened the door and greeted the guests and led them to the kitchen where Mom was.

"Hello, Janelle. How are you today?" Mom smiled welcomingly.

"We are fine. Thank you. We have a surprise to share with your family later tonight, but I will tell you now." Mrs. Share whispered the secret in Mom's ear and when she finished Mom squealed with excitement, "Oh, Janelle, congratulations! I'm so happy for you."

Martha looked questioningly at her Mom but she only said, "You'll find out later."

Martha thought to herself, *I wonder what they are being so secretive about? Well, I'll just have to find out later.*

"Okay, I think we are ready. Martha, would you go call the others and tell them we are ready and to meet us on the porch in two minutes, please?" asked Mom.

"Sure, Mom," replied Martha.

Two minutes later, everyone met on the porch.

"Okay, let's head out, everyone!" said Dad.

They started out two by two. Dad and Mr. Share in the lead, Mom and Mrs. Share following, talking about their 'secret,' Thomas and James, then Anna and Sarah, Lydia and Martha, with Elizabeth on her hip took the rear. The girls all followed at a distance, taking it slow, for the path to the river was kind of rough, especially for Sarah's short legs.

About ten minutes later, the family and their guests arrived at the desired spot. Mrs. Share and Mom laid out the picnic while the kids waded in the river with Dad and Mr. Share watching closely.

About another ten minutes later, Mom called them to supper and everyone gathered around the picnic blanket. Everyone joined hands to pray, but first Pastor Share spoke up, "Before we pray, I would like to make a little announcement. My lovely wife found out Friday, and I am completely thrilled that we are going to be first-time parents by early March!"

"That's wonderful! Congratulations!" said Dad shaking Pastor Share's hand.

"Yes, we are very excited," he replied looking at his wife tenderly.

"So THAT'S what you were giggling and squealing about earlier. I'm so happy for you, Mrs. Share. I can't wait to grow up, get married and have children... if that's what God's plan for me is, of course." Martha grinned dreamily.

"Yes, it's a blessing, and a lot of fun, but don't desire to grow up too fast. These years are precious. Hold on to them. You'll never forget these single years." The look in Mrs. Share's eyes was loving and Martha knew her Mom's friend would be a great mother.

"Thanks for the advice, Mrs. Share. I'll remember that," said Martha.

After Martha, Anna and Lydia were finished with their dinner, Martha asked if they could go make flower chains from the flowers around the river. Mom gave them permission, so the girls scurried off to find some flowers that were in the sight of the parents so the adults could watch out for any trouble. And things continued this way the rest of the evening.

Chapter 4
Wild Wagon Ride

It was Friday. Martha came in from doing her morning chores. "Good morning, Mom!"
"Good morning, Martha. Did you sleep well?"

"Yes, where's Sarah?" Martha noticed the table wasn't set, and that was Sarah's job.

"She's not feeling very well. Anna and Lydia are both keeping an eye on Elizabeth."

"Oh, okay. I'll set the table for you," volunteered Martha.

"Thank you, Martha. You're a great help," replied Mom.

About five minutes later Dad came in; his eyes were swollen and he was sniffling a lot. "I don't feel so well."

"Oh sweetheart, I'm sorry," said Mom as she went over and felt his head. "Yes, I do believe you have a fever. You need to go back to bed and rest." Mom led him to the stairs.

"I can't. There's work to do and today I have to go to the market," Dad protested.

"Martha can do that and the boys can take care of the chores," said Mom. "I'll even send Anna with Martha."

"I guess that's okay, but be careful, Martha," agreed Dad looking at his eldest daughter.

"I will, Dad. I promise," replied Martha.

Dad headed upstairs and just then the boys asked, "Where's Dad going?"

"Back to bed; he isn't feeling too well," replied Mom.

"Oh," said both boys sadly. Martha wondered if they were more worried about Dad or about having to do extra chores.

A mother knows these things. "Now, boys, please don't complain. Sarah is sick as well, and Martha and Anna are going to the store right after breakfast and I have Lydia and Elizabeth to tend to."

"Yes ma'am," for they suddenly felt sorry for their Mom and offered to help her.

"Yes, I would love your help, boys. Would you mind watering and weeding the garden for me?"

Although that chore was not their favorite, they agreed to do it with no more complaints.

After breakfast and the dishes were done, the

boys hitched up the horses, Vernon and Zoe. About ten minutes later Martha and Anna were ready to go.

They kissed their mother, who was secretly concerned about their safety; but assuring herself that it was perfectly safe, she tried not to worry. "Good-bye, please be careful!"

"We will, Mom," replied Martha as she clucked to the horses and slapped the reins.

In about two hours, Martha tied the horses to a hitching post and she and Anna went to the market to get the things Mom would need. She picked out baking powder, salt, and sugar.

Before long it was time to check out. Martha had her pocket money with her and when she saw Anna looking at the peppermint sticks, she decided she would bless her sister by buying her a stick. "Two peppermint sticks, please," said Martha handing him two cents.

After they put the groceries in the wagon, Martha and Anna climbed up and went to the mill where they sold logs their father had chopped down. "Hi. Mr. Gershon. My Dad's sick so we girls came instead."

"Oh, that's mighty nice of ya," said Mr. Gershon.

"I would help you if I could, Mr. Gershon, but I am afraid I'm not strong enough."

"Well, I suspected that," Mr. Gershon said teasingly. "I'll have my helper, John, help me unload it."

"Thank you, Mr. Gershon. My sister and I will be over there," Martha pointed to the water wheel.

"Okay, I'll tell ya when we're finished," replied Mr. Gershon.

Martha and Anna went to watch the water wheel and suck on their peppermint sticks and before long Mr. Gershon and John were done.

"Well there ya go," said Mr. Gershon, handing Martha an envelope with money in it.

"Okay, thanks, Mr. Gershon."

John came around and just when Martha was about to step up on the wagon, John offered his hand and Martha took it. "Thank you," she said smiling at him. John did the same with Anna, except she giggled and Martha had to remind her to thank him.

They were almost home when something seemed to bother the horses. As they picked up the speed, Martha tried to slow them down but they did quite the opposite. Martha pulled back on the reigns hard, but that didn't deter the horses any.

"WHOA! Vernon, WHOA! Zoe. Easy girl. Come on, slow down." By this time Anna was pale with fear and Martha was trying to keep from panicking.

Now the wagon was swaying and the horses were not even on the road anymore. They were running in the meadow!

Suddenly Martha spied something and saw it looked like a young man. As they got closer she saw it was Samuel Poltor. She yelled with all her might at the figure who was apparently taking the long walk home.

"SAMUEL POLTOR! OVER HERE!" cried Martha. Anna was crying now and clinging to Martha's right arm. She called again and Samuel looked up, surprised to see two girls in the wagon. He heard a familiar voice and recognized it belonged to Martha Knight. He waited for the wagon to get close and when it did he stretched out his strong arm and grabbed the horses by the halter. When he stopped them he was clearly out of breath. Martha got down and helped Anna down and said, "Oh thank you, Mr. Poltor! I thought we were goners!"

Samuel smiled, "No need for that Mr. Poltor stuff. I'm Samuel to you and your family and always will be. Are you both all right?"

Martha blushed. "Thank you. We're both
fine. The ride just gave us a scare."

"You're welcome; I'm glad you're both okay.
Where's your dad? Doesn't he usually make the
ride to town?"

"Yes, he does, but he and Sarah are sick. The
boys are home doing the chores, so Mom had Anna
and me go to town."

"Oh, okay," he said, relieved that their father
wasn't hurt or anything.

"Well the least we can do is offer you a ride
home," said Martha.

"Well, that would be very nice, Martha.
Thank you," replied Samuel.

Martha and Anna climbed back on the wagon
and Samuel squeezed in beside Anna. Martha
clucked to the horses and they started. It was about
fifteen more minutes before they got to the Poltor
house and when Martha told the story, Mrs. Poltor
said, "Oh, you poor dears. Would you like to have
supper with us? It will be on in about an hour."

"No; but thank you, ma'am. My Mom is
probably worried sick about us. We are already
about an hour overdue, but thank you for the

offer."

"Oh, I'm sorry, Martha. I didn't realize you were due to get home or I would have never accepted your invitation for a ride home," said Samuel, worried.

"Oh nonsense, the least we could do was to offer you a ride home. My Mom would get me for not offering," replied Martha.

"Well, if you say so. Thank you again," replied Samuel with a short bow.

"Oh, my pleasure," smiled Martha. "Thank you for stopping the wagon. I'm sure God sent you."

"Actually, Martha, I was going to go on the road, but something told me to go through the meadow. It truly must have been the Holy Spirit."

"Well, I'm very thankful He sent you," replied Martha.

"I am too," said Samuel.

"Well, we'd better get home or Mom is going to come looking for us, horses or no horses," Martha joked.

Everyone laughed with her and bid the girls farewell.

By the time Martha and Anna got home, Mom was standing on the porch with a worried expression on her face. When they pulled up she said, "Oh, Martha, I was so worried!"

"It's a long story. I'll tell you over supper. By the way what *is* for supper? We're hungry!"

Mom laughed, relieved everything was all right.

Over supper, the family stared in rapt attention as Martha began, "Well first, we got all that was on the list, but on the ride home......"

Chapter 5
New Child of the King

Martha woke the next morning feeling not so well. Instead of getting up and ready for a new day, she walked downstairs in her nightgown. Mom sensed something was wrong at once. "Martha? Are you not feeling well?"

"N-no," she coughed. "No, I don't. I have a headache and my throat is sore and I have this cough." She coughed again.

"Oh, this illness keeps passing from person to person. Well, you need to get back to bed, young lady. I'll have Anna and the boys cover your chores for a while. Now, back to bed," said Mom again as she guided her back towards the stairs and tucked her back into bed. "You stay here and I'll bring you some warm milk and porridge once the boys come back with the milk."

"O-okay," croaked Martha as she coughed again.

"I think we may have to send for the doctor if it gets any worse--yours seems the worst so far. I'm going to move the other girls out of this room and hopefully no one else will get sick." Mom made sure Martha was all tucked in and then left the room saying, "Try to go back to sleep. Sleep is good for sickness."

Mom headed downstairs and started some porridge. "Anna, I would like you to go and feed the chickens. Martha isn't feeling well right now and please tell the boys to rake out the stalls, I'm going to bring some of this porridge to her and Sarah." said Mom.

"Okay, Mom," Anna agreed as she headed out the door.

About ten o'clock a.m. the doctor arrived with his black bag in hand and followed Mom into the girls' bedroom. After a full examination the doctor pronounced Martha very sick and gave Mom some medicine and said, "Keep her calm and keep the covers over her, no matter how hot she gets. Give her this medicine every two hours. Her recovery will be slow, but I suggest a week off work would be fine until she's up and about. Call me if she gets considerably worse."

"We will, Dr. Barns. Tell Angela hi for me. Be careful," replied Mom.

"I will," Dr. Barns.

"Have a good day, doctor," Mom smiled gratefully at Dr. Barns as he turned to go.

"Thank you, you too," Paul Barns replied.

Monday, Martha woke up feeling much better, but still weak. She needed to stay in bed for at least another day. Martha decided to read her Bible before breakfast. She grabbed her Bible from the nightstand and opened it up to Philippians 4:8 *"Finally, brethren, whatsoever things are* **true***, whatsoever things are honest, whatsoever things are just, whatsoever things are pure, whatsoever things are lovely, whatsoever things are of good report; if there be any virtue, and if there be any praise, think on these things."*

I suppose this means I shouldn't think ill of somebody else, or have any inappropriate thoughts. I'm going to try very hard on thinking pure and praiseworthy things. Martha prayed silently, *Dear Father in Heaven, Thank You for this day. I'm still very weak, but I believe You have a purpose for me getting sick. Thank You again Lord for protecting Anna and me Friday during that crazy and wild wagon ride. I know You sent Samuel Poltor to us. Thank You for your blessings. Amen.*

Just as Martha finished praying she heard a knock on the door.

"Come in," said Martha. The door opened and there stood Anna.

"Good morning, Anna. How are you feeling this morning?"

"I'm feeling fine. Mom wanted me to bring this oatmeal and warm milk up to you. How are you feeling?"

"I'm actually feeling much better. I think I will be back to normal by tomorrow," said Martha.

"Do you mind if I stay here while you eat?" asked Anna.

"Sure. I don't mind at all," Martha patted a spot on the bed. "Come and sit on the bed with me. I don't think I am contagious anymore."

"Okay, thanks, Martha," replied Anna.

For some reason Martha felt that Anna was a bit troubled but she felt the Holy Spirit tell her to wait—*wait a few minutes, she'll tell you what's wrong if you say nothing for a minute or two.*

Inwardly Martha said, *Okay, Holy Spirit, thank You.*

There was an awkward silence that followed but Martha just ignored it and waited. Suddenly, Anna spoke with much feeling in her voice.

"Where do you go when you die?" asked Anna.

"Well," started Martha, "the Bible tells us that we have to confess and ask Jesus Christ into our hearts to go to Heaven."

"But... what if, uh, w-we d-don't?" asked Anna, fidgeting on her apron string.

"Well, sadly, many people believe that we can get to Heaven by good works. Say that I go and weed out our neighbor's garden and I say to myself afterwards, 'I did a good deed. Surely God will let me into Heaven.' But it doesn't work that way. God says in His word that we are all guilty of sin and the gift of salvation is our only way into Heaven."

Martha reached for her Bible once again and quoted, "1 John 1:9 says, that if we confess our sins He —that is God— He is faithful and just to forgive us our sins and cleanse us from all unrighteousness."

Martha paused for a minute to look up at Anna's face which was deep in thought. "Also, Anna, John 3:16 says, *'For God so loved the world, that He gave His only begotten Son, that whosoever believeth in Him should not perish, but have everlasting life.'*"

"God really loves me that much?" asked Anna.

"Yes, He loves us so much that He sent His Son to be nailed on a cross to die for OUR sins! Now isn't He a great God? Not only is He our God, He is our Daddy who loves us. God just lent us children to our parents for a little while just like He'll lend us our future children if it's His plan for us to marry and have children someday."

"I've heard these verses before, but I guess I never really thought about them a lot. How do you become a Christian, Martha?"

"The Bible says that if you confess with your mouth that Jesus Christ is Lord and that He raised from the dead, you'll be saved and a born again Christian," said Martha.

"Can I ask Him to be my Lord and come into my heart right now?" asked Anna.

"Certainly, why don't you go and ask Mom to pray with you? Ask her to come up here so I can be with you too!" said Martha excitedly.

"Okay, Martha. Thank you!"

"It's not me that needs thanking. It's our precious Lord you need to thank, not me," said Martha smiling.

About five to ten minutes later a new babe was born into the Kingdom of God!

Chapter 6
Guest Over Dinner

Martha woke Tuesday morning feeling much better. She got up and dressed, made her bed, and braided her hair. She went out in the nice brisk morning air. *What a glorious day it is! Thank You, God, for this day. Let me use it to Your glory.* Martha went into the barn and greeted her brothers good morning. Then she started raking out the stalls.

"How are you feeling?" asked James.

"I'm feeling much better. Thank you," replied Martha.

"Would you like to go fishing with Thomas and me this afternoon, after lunch?"

"Thank you, but—" before she could finish James interrupted her.

"I'll bait and even get the hook out for you," said James, insistently.

"Well...okay, thank you," said Martha.

"Yippee!" yelped James.

Martha smiled to herself. She hadn't realized her brothers had missed her while she'd been ill. "Well, I'd better go and feed the chickens. Mom will need the eggs." She put her rake up and headed for the chicken coop with some food in her apron.

After breakfast, Martha went to help with the dishes and she asked, "Mom, can I go fishing with the boys this afternoon after lunch?"

"Well, I suppose you can, but I will need you to complete some tasks before lunch if you want to go fishing," replied Mom.

"Okay. Give me the tasks and I'll finish them BEFORE lunch," said Martha with extra enthusiasm.

Mom wrote down the tasks that she needed Martha to do.

The list read:
1. *Start making invitations*
2. *Sweep the girls' room*
3. *Rake the yard*
4. *Clean living room windows*

"Okay, thanks," Martha said, hugging Mom around the waist.

Martha hurried to the living room and sat down at a little desk by a window. She got some pieces of paper out and started writing in her best penmanship.

Dear Williams Family,

You are invited to a party! Peter and Rosemary Knight are renewing their vows and the Knight family is inviting you to attend! When: August 24th starting at 4:00, until 9:00. Where: In the Knight's yard.

Please let us know if you can attend! We hope you can!

Love and Blessings,
The Knight family

Martha repeated this for the McShire family, Poltor family, Gates family, Doctor Paul and Angela Barns, Kate family, and lastly, Grandma and Grandpa Knight, who lived about fifteen miles from the Knight family. "That should be enough for today."

Martha went to her room with the broom. She opened the door and to her dismay she saw that the girls' room was very messy. "ANNA and LYDIA KNIGHT! Come here right NOW!" There was the sound of feet hurrying up the steps and a moment later they appeared in the room.

"Why is our room like this?" asked Martha harshly.

"We're sorry, Martha," spoke Anna for both of them, for Lydia was too overwrought to speak.

"This morning we were playing before breakfast. We had Mom's permission. We must have forgotten to pick up. Oh, now I remember, Mom called us to breakfast when we were only half done with cleaning up," said Anna. Lydia only nodded her head.

Martha, her anger cooling down a bit, said, "Anna, Lydia, please forgive me for yelling and losing my temper. I had no right to yell and I need to work on my self-control. Will you please forgive me?" asked Martha.

"Sure, Martha, we forgive you. The Bible says when someone asks forgiveness, we need to forgive them," said Anna. Lydia squeaked out a "yes."

"Thank you. I'll try very hard to do better," replied Martha.

Anna and Lydia quickly set about cleaning the room so Martha could sweep.

After Martha had swept, she moved on to raking the leaves. She had them all in a nice pile when three-year-old Sarah jumped right into them. Martha felt anger bubbling within her, but before she yelled at her, she thought, *It's not a big mess. I just need to ask her politely to not jump in the leaf pile anymore.*

"Sarah, would you mind not jumping in my leaf pile again, please?" asked Martha kindly.

"Yes, Marta, I won't jump in your pile anymore. Mom is hangin' clothes on da line wight now."

"Okay, you can sit by the leaf pile if you want. I'm almost finished," said Martha kindly, glad she chose the right way to handle things.

Martha was reminded about the conversation she had had with Mary just a few weeks prior to this incident. She smiled to herself, glad she handled the situation better than she had the one previously.

After Martha cleaned the windows, it was time for lunch. Thomas, James, and Dad came in and washed up and a few minutes later everyone was sitting around the table. "Let's pray," said Dad, bowing his head and folding his hands.

"Dear Father in Heaven, Thank You for this food you have provided for us. Thank You for this wonderful family you have given me. Let us use this afternoon to Your will. Amen."

Everyone started passing around plates of peanut butter and jelly sandwiches and meat sandwiches and started eating. It was a fairly quiet meal. Everyone absorbed in his or her own thoughts until suddenly Mom spoke up. "Martha, Thomas, and James, I would like you back home from fishing by three o'clock because the Gates family is coming over and should be here by five o'clock. I'll need both Martha's and Anna's help with supper and I think you boys should do your chores earlier than usual so you can play with Bruce and Fred."

"Yes ma'am," said both boys in unison, excited that the Gates family would be coming over for supper. Though the Gates boys were much older, Thomas and James really looked up to them and enjoyed spending time with them.

After lunch, and the dishes were done and put away, Thomas, James, and Martha grabbed their fishing poles and headed out the back door. As usual, they closed it carefully to avoid waking the little ones.

The fishing pond was just about a quarter of a mile across the fields and across the meadow. The stream the Knights had gone to a couple weekends ago ended up at this pond.

When they got to the perfect spot, Martha sat down and the boys went off to find bait.

Martha gazed up at the afternoon blue sky. *How mighty God is to create such a beautiful sky.*

The boys were soon back with several plump worms and they decided, since Martha was the girl, they would bait hers first. James baited Martha's hook. Just when James was about to cast it into the water, Martha stood up and said a little shyly, "If you don't mind, I would like to cast the pole, please."

"Well, certainly, me madam. Me lady has a right to her own pole," James said with an exaggerated accent.

Martha laughed heartily at her silly brother, and threw her line in and sat down. Not many minutes later she felt a tug. She almost gasped. "Boys, I felt a tug."

Laying his pole down, James stood up and came up behind her. "Eek, I felt it again."

"Calm down. Keep a cool head and bring him in. I'll catch him with this net when he's out of the water," James chuckled while holding out the net.

Martha calmed herself down and started to reel the fish in.

It felt to Martha like five whole minutes had passed, but was really about ten seconds later when she pulled a huge fish in triumphantly.

"Wow! It's a whopper, Martha!" James took the hook out and laid the fish in the water tied to a stick. But just when James sat back down, his pole leaped out of the water. James went in the water to get his pole back and got all wet in the midst of trying to get it. One time he slipped and fell, but still he fought to get it back.

Finally he had to face it that his pole was gone.

Martha felt awful. That pole was his most prized possession, other than his Bible. He'd gotten it for his eighth birthday, and now he'd lost it because of her.

Martha went up to her brother and wrapped her arms around him, causing the front of her dress to get wet. "I'm so sorry, James. I know you loved that pole very much. And you lost it all because of me."

James nodded, tears in his eyes though he tried to choke them down. "I-it's okay, M-Martha, I -it w-wasn't y-your fault. D-don't f-feel b-bad."

But Martha did feel awful.

Meanwhile, Thomas, who had caught a big fish, looked sadly at his distraught brother. Taking care of the fish, he said, "You can share my pole, James. I'm sorry about what happened to yours. Wait—maybe I can still find it."

"No, Thomas," sniffled James, brushing his arm across his eyes. "It's no use; it's gone. Thank you for offering anyway."

"Why don't you try my pole? We still have

some fish to catch," stated Thomas, with an added look of sympathy toward his brother.

"No thanks. You and Martha go ahead and fish, I'm gonna go to the house and get dried off." Thomas and Martha looked at each other, and the young boy nodded; they'd go to the house with their brother. Gathering their fish, they trooped to the house with James.

By the time they got to the house, James was lagging far behind, still trying to regain his composure.

Since James was out of sight when they came up to the house, Mom looked concerned. "What happened? Where is James?"

Martha's face sagged even more. "He's coming. He lost his pole in the pond because of me. He was helping me unhook the fish from my pole and when he sat back down to fish, the pole leapt up with a fish tugging at it and now it's gone, all because of me. I didn't know I could cause this much trouble."

Before her mom could say a word, Martha headed up to her room to change into a different dress. Then she got out her money from a little box under her bed and counted it. *I have enough money! On Friday when Dad goes to town I'll ask him if I can join him and pick out the nicest pole I can find. I think I have enough money to by him a nice one.*

Martha put her money away, smoothed her skirt and went downstairs to help her mom prepare for their guests. When Mom saw her, she swept her up in a big hug. "I know you didn't mean to cause James' fishing pole to be lost. I know it hurts you terribly, but James is handling it great, so you don't need to be sad."

Martha smiled and told her mother about her plan to get him a new pole and when she finished Mom exclaimed, "How very unselfish and kind of you. That's a wonderful idea."

"Then may I have permission to go to town with Dad on Friday, just him and me?" asked Martha hopefully.

"Well, let me speak to your Father first, but I think that will be all right. Would you please set the table? It's already nearly four o'clock and I want everything ready so I can chat with Mrs. Gates before dinner."

"Sure, Mom," Martha replied happily.

At five-o'clock sharp there was a hard knock on the door. Mom hurriedly took off her apron and hung it in the pantry and went to greet the guests. She beckoned the adults to come out on the porch where there was just a light breeze to cool them off.

Bruce and Fred Gates, along with the four oldest Knight children, all went under the big oak just west of the house. They sat down and started talking about what they should do that evening. James piped up, "How about we go down to the river and wade? It's so humid that it makes your head swim."

"That's a great idea, James," said Martha, "how about it, Bruce and Fred?"

"We think it's a swell plan," said both boys.

Just then they all heard Mom calling them in for supper, so they all went in to eat. After the prayer was said, the adults started talking.

"I hear the economy is getting worse. Ever since the Depression began there's talk that it might affect us and our farms. It's just-" but as quickly as Mr. Gates started, he was cut off by Dad even faster.

"Jim," started Dad, "can we please talk about this another time?"

"Oh, I'm sorry, Peter. I keep forgetting you have younger ones here. We can talk of this later."

"Thank you," said Dad.

Martha was already disturbed. *I heard about this Depression, but are things really THIS bad?*

Will the economy decline affect us? If so, how much? But Martha quickly put these unanswered questions in the back of her mind, because just then, Fred asked a question.

The rest of the time spent together was fun and relaxing, and Martha didn't think of the disturbing event in history the rest of the night.

Chapter 7
Family Picnic

Saturday afternoon was a bit humid but otherwise it was a glorious day and the Knight family decided to have a picnic before it got too hot. They all decided they should picnic by the pond and also do some fishing. If they caught enough, Mom would cook some up for supper.

The day before, Martha had found the perfect pole for her brother. Dad had given her a proud smile of approval and she beamed at his attention.

James, who had been thrilled to get a new fishing pole, couldn't stop thanking Martha. She was just glad she could make it up to her brother.

The family started out walking at about eleven o'clock, with Dad and the boys leading, Anna, Lydia, and Sarah in the middle and Mom, with Elizabeth on her hip, and Martha bringing up the rear with their Great Pyrenees they called Nellie. Martha thought this would be the best time to bring up a question that had been bothering her.

"Mom," she started, "will the Depression affect us?"

This question took Mom by surprise. Taking considerable thought on how much to tell her, she said, "Well, everything is pretty bad, but, as farmers, I believe we are much safer than the business workers. We are no exception though. We need the mill to buy our wood we chopped and the seed and corn we grow so we can have money. So to answer your question, yes, we can be affected by the Depression. We just need to pray that God will protect us and all the other farmers." She withheld the fact that the price for the wood they sold to the mill was getting lower by the month.

This seemed to satisfy Martha, and she was quiet the rest of the trip.

Once the Knight family got to their destination, everyone set about on their adventures. James was very eager to try out his new fishing pole. Thomas began scanning the air for hawks and other birds with his pair of binoculars, and Mom settled Elizabeth on a blanket. Anna and Sarah decided to look for leaves that they could print on paper to make cards. Lydia and Martha decided to make flower chains.

Soon after their arrival, Mom called them all to lunch. Martha and Lydia ran to the blanket first. They sat down and helped Mom hand out the sandwiches and canteens of lemonade and water. "Martha, would you pour the drinks for me, please?" asked Mom.

"Sure." Martha reached for the stack of cups. She asked what people wanted and poured three glasses of lemonade and five glasses of water.

About ten minutes later, Martha was just finishing up her last sandwich when she heard a noise in the tall grasses. *Hmm, I wonder what that could be,* pondered Martha. She decided to go and look. She got her parent's permission, and with Lydia, Thomas and Nellie trailing her to see what it was, Martha set off. As soon as she reached the grasses, they heard the sound again. Now she was getting excited and she had to admit, a bit nervous.

Martha started pulling away the tall bits of grass to make her way when the noise sounded again, louder now. Martha thought she heard a faint crying. When she was about to give up and turn back she saw a flash of white. This time, Martha tried to run and catch it, but the grass was slowing her down. She was just about to give up again when the little unknown creature bounded up and into Martha's arms. Before she could even say that it was the cutest kitten she'd ever seen, Nellie started running circles around Martha's legs, yelping wildly.

"Stop that right now, Nellie! Sit," she commanded. The excited dog stopped and sat down on her haunches. With a sorrowful, begging face, she fought the urge to start whining.

"Oh, the poor little tyke; let's take him to Mom and check and see if he has any injuries," Martha told her siblings.

About ten minutes later, Mom announced

that the little kitten was unharmed and when Martha asked to keep him she answered, "Well, Martha, we need to post around town that we found a kitten and if no one answers after one month, then you may keep her. I happened to look and I saw 'he' is actually a girl."

"Oh. Can I name her?" asked Martha, trying not to get too excited.

"Sorry, Martha, I'm going to say no because if she has an owner that means she has a name. After one month, if no one comes for her, then you may name her and keep her."

"Okay, Mom," said Martha, clearly disappointed. But then she perked up and said, "I sure hope I can keep him. I mean her."

"Well, we'll see," said Mom, smiling at Martha's enthusiasm. It wasn't much later that afternoon Dad called them for dessert. "Hooray!" cheered the children.

Later that evening, after a delicious supper of fish that James had caught and Mom had fried, Martha sat at the kitchen table working on some posters. Thomas and James sat in the corner playing checkers. Anna and Lydia were looking at a picture book. Dad was reading to Sarah. Elizabeth was on a blanket on the floor and Mom was in her rocking chair knitting.

Martha drew a picture of a cat playing with a ball of yarn and wrote:

Found Cat:

A white cat with blue eyes with one ear up and one turned down.

Please contact Peter and Rosemary Knight. They live in Helena, Montana about fifteen miles west out of town.

After she finished printing the others, she decided to go to bed earlier than usual since she was worn out. She bid her parents and siblings good night and headed up the stairs. She slipped into her night gown and undid her hair and put it in her night cap. She washed her face and brushed her teeth. Then she got her diary out and a pen and started writing.

July 11th 1930

Dear God,

Today, my family and I went on a family picnic. It was so much fun! I found a little kitten. Mom says I have to wait a month to see if anyone comes to claim her. Oh, I do so hope I can keep her. If it's Your will, please let me keep her. But, if not, please help me to have a good attitude about it. Well, I'm very tired. I think I better get to bed.

Love, Your servant,

Martha Rosemary Knight

Martha put her diary and pen away and hopped into the bed that she shared with Anna. Looking toward the window she prayed, *Please, God, let me keep her.*

Chapter 8
Party

It was Wednesday, July 15th, and Martha was just taking a break from cleaning the yard for the upcoming party. She decided to check the mail and got up from the porch, setting her cool glass of lemonade down on the railing. She started at a brisk walk and about five minutes later was pulling the mail from the mail box. She saw her name on one of the envelopes, from her good friend Cathryn Williams, and hurried back to the porch to read it.

Once she got there she tore open the paper and read:

Dear Martha,

I would like to invite you to come over to our house for a party. There will be some other girls from church going, and also my cousin, Irene, who is visiting from Colorado. The sleep over is Friday and people can start arriving at three o'clock. I sincerely hope you can join us.

Love, your dear friend,

Cathryn Williams.

P.S. There is going to be cake and ice cream too!

Martha smiled happily, folded up the letter

and put it in her apron pocket. She would ask her parents later that night. She put the mail inside the house in the mail bin and started getting back to work.

Knock-knock...knock. The door opened and Mrs. Williams greeted Martha with a smile.

"Welcome, Martha. The girls are in the living room. Please follow me." Mrs. Williams smiled and nodded to Mr. Knight.

Martha and her father followed Mrs. Williams into the living room where several girls were gathered. Cathryn and Rose Williams, and Polly and Selah McShire, Mary Poltor and Jane Kate all smiled at Martha.

"Miss Knight has arrived," said Mrs. Williams.

All the girls got up and surrounded Martha with giggles and little hugs.

"Martha," Dad said, "it's 3:15 right now. I'll pick you up at 11:30 a.m. tomorrow."

"Yes sir," replied Martha. She gave her dad a quick hug and peck on the cheek.

After Dad left, the girls gathered around the table. Cathryn laid out a quilt and Rose got her needle and some thread for the other girls who brought their own needles.

They started talking as they sewed and Cathryn and Rose introduced their cousin, Irene Williams, who was visiting from Colorado for a month.

Then Cathryn brought up a subject that bothered Martha. "My Dad isn't getting any money from the logs he sells to the mills anymore. They just can't pay them anymore and the price for the wheat has gone down considerably." Several of the girls nodded their heads knowingly but Martha just sat there, needle in midair with a worried expression on her face.

I wonder how we are faring. Does this problem include us? Is this that Depression again?

The girls had moved on to another subject so Martha turned her attention to what they were talking about, but the worry she felt did not completely go away.

Supper came, and as the girls were going along the counter, dishing up their food in the buffet style, Irene Williams piped up, "So Martha, how far do you live from here?"

"Oh, not far," said Martha, dishing some corn onto her plate, "probably about fifteen minutes. You live in Colorado, right?"

"Yes. I live there with my parents and four siblings."

"That's great. I live with my dad, mom, and six siblings; two boys and four girls."

"You must have a lot of fun; I know I have fun playing with my siblings. Are you the oldest?"

"Yes. I'm twelve. How about you?" asked Martha curiously.

"I just turned thirteen; when's your birthday?"

"October fifth; what's yours?"

"June fifteenth."

Irene and Martha finished filling their plates and they went together to the table where a very nice conversation ensued between them.

Supper was eaten with relish, and then they all adjourned to the living room where Rose offered to read to the girls while some quietly listened, and some worked some more on their sewing, while still others drew.

The rest of the evening passed quite delightfully, and before Martha knew it, it was the next day and her father came to pick her up.

It was about 9:30 that night and Martha had long gone to bed. Anna was sleeping soundly beside her, Lydia and Sarah in the next bed, and Elizabeth in the bassinet in the corner of the room. Martha could hear her parents talking downstairs in the living room. Just when Martha thought she couldn't bear the worry that left her in a fright any longer, she quietly pulled the covers away as to not to wake her sisters and, crept downstairs and entered the living room.

Seeing their daughter at such a late hour, her parents were a bit shaken. "Are you feeling all right, Martha? What's wrong, dear?" asked Mom, seeing the distraught look on Martha's face.

Martha walked in front of her mother and father and blurted out, "Cathryn said that the price for wheat is going down and that the mill owners are not able to pay for the logs that people sell them. Is this true?"

"Ah, yes, Martha, we are not getting paid anymore for the wood and the price for the wheat has gone down. Both are true, but we really have no cause for worry yet. God is taking care of us. And not getting paid for the wood could turn out to be not a curse but a blessing. We'll have a lot of extra wood for winter."

"Yes," said Martha, nodding slowly.

Mom held Martha's face in her hands and looked into her eyes: "Oh, sweet girl. I'm sorry you heard about this, but maybe it's for the best. Please do not tell your siblings. I don't want them worried, too."

"Yes ma'am," Martha replied solemnly.

"Hey, Martha, don't be afraid. Mom's right— God's already taking care of us. Your Mother's garden is very plentiful this year, thanks to you and your sisters. Would you feel better if we prayed?" asked Dad.

"Y-yes, Dad. I'd like that," answered Martha.

"Okay, then let us pray." Dad grasped Martha's and Mom's hands, and the three bowed their heads as he led them in prayer. "Dear Jesus, We come to You now and we thank You for Your care and protection. We are very thankful. We ask You to please bless the mill people and protect them too. Please protect us in our sleep tonight and thank You. Amen."

After a long warm hug from her parents, Martha went back to bed and slept peacefully all the night through.

Chapter 9
Plans Set in Motion

Martha woke with a start. "Today is the day!" she squealed. "It has been a month since I found the little kitten, and today is when I can keep her." Martha jumped out of the bed and ran downstairs and into the kitchen where Mom was cooking breakfast. "Where is my kitten?" asked Martha.

"The last time I saw her she was behind the wood box sleeping," Mom replied.

"Okay, Mom," said Martha, as she turned and hurried to the wood box. "Oh, you're still here," she cooed as she picked up the kitten and cradled her in her arms.

"Wow! The time has really flown by. I hadn't realized that today is a month since you found her. I guess that means you can keep her," smiled Mom.

"I think I will name her Jubilee," said Martha, "because she was found bouncing and running."

"That's a good name, but you need to get dressed and do your chores. Have you noticed you are still wearing your night gown and cap?"

"Oh, I am, aren't I?"

"Hmm-hmm," said Mom with a playful smile on her face.

"Well, I guess I should get upstairs then," laughed Martha.

"Yes and scoot," teased Mom, poking Martha with the clean spoon she was holding.

It was about a week later, August 15th, and Martha had just finished the last placement card for the quickly approaching party. Martha heard a knock at the door. "I'll get it!" she said. She walked to the door and opened it to see a young mom and a little girl.

"Hello. How may I help you?" asked Martha, wondering who they were.

"Thank you. We are so sorry to bother you, and it might be too late, but my daughter, Ashley, lost her little kitten and we just saw a poster that was made. It's already been a month, so we'll understand if you've already given her away or adopted her as your own, but Ashley would really like her back."

"Wait just a minute please," Martha showed them into the living room and went to find Ashley's kitten. She could barely breathe as she knelt in the kitchen where she had seen Jubilee last. *God, I don't want to give Jubilee up, but I know that's what You would want me to do, and I also know that I would want the same for me if I had a lost pet. Help me to do the right thing. And help it not be so very hard. Amen.*

Martha went to the window where she'd last seen Jubilee. She found her and cuddled her one last time and said, "Your owner has come for you and I know I'm doing the right thing, but I will miss you so much."

Martha carried the little kitten to the living room, knelt on one knee, and handed the kitten to the little girl. Here you go. I have taken good care of her for you. If I'd lost a kitten, I know I would want that someone to do the same for me as I'm doing for you. She's a really nice and pretty kitten." Martha smiled and tried to look happy.

"Oh, Liberty!" Ashley smiled her sweetest and biggest smile and took the kitten in one hand and grabbed Martha's hand with the other. "Thank you so much. It's very kind of you. I'll do the same for any missing pet I find," said Ashley.

"I'm sure you will. Will you write me and tell me how she is doing in say about a week or so? I really would like to hear how she is doing," Martha said.

"Sure, I'd be happy to!" Ashley agreed happily.

"I appreciate that, and my name, by the way, is Martha. And I have a sister named Lydia who I know would love to be your pen pal. Would you like that?"

"Oh yes," said Ashley.

"Well, we'd better go. Thank you so much. We have a lot to be grateful for," Ashley's Mom said.

"Oh, you're welcome," Martha told her, trying to hide her disappointment and hold in the tears that she felt like crying. As Ashley and her mother left, Martha watched them for a minute, long enough to see Ashley turn back and wave at her. Martha waved back, went into the house and to her parents' bedroom. Her mom was folding clothes and watching Elizabeth play on the bed. Martha was pale and clearly upset. Mom went to her and put an arm around her. "What is it Martha? What's wrong?" Martha spilled out the whole story and at the end she was crying.

"Oh, I'm so proud of you. And I'm sorry that you had to go through this, but I know you're stronger for it."

"Yes, I know I am, but it's hard. She was my only own pet until now."

"I know. I know. But I'm still proud of you."

"Thanks, Mom. I think I'll run into town to the grocery store and shop for the ingredients we'll need to make the food with. It's only ten o'clock now. I can get back by four if that's alright with you," requested Martha.

"Sure you can. Pack some lunches. I want you to take Thomas with you; you can catch him if you hurry. I think he came back from the fields about a minute ago to get a drink of water."

"Okay, Mom," replied Martha as she hurried out to the pump where Thomas was pouring water over his head. "Hey Thomas, would you like to go to town with me? I'm going to shop for the party food."

"Sure. Let me go tell Dad and James and change into some clean clothes. Then I'll hitch up the horses while you make some sack lunches. Give me about fifteen minutes and then we'll get going," said Thomas hurrying back to the fields.

Martha headed back to the kitchen and made peanut butter and jam sandwiches. She got some strawberries and wrapped them up, filled a canteen with ice and lemonade and packed the sandwiches and strawberries into a sack. She went out to put the sack and canteen into the wagon and then ran back inside. Upstairs in the girls' room, she got the shopping list, making sure the money they needed was in the envelope, and slipped it into her apron pocket.

Martha said a quick good-bye to Mom and hurried outside where Thomas was waiting for her.

As they began moving, Martha told him what had happened with Jubilee/Liberty and when she finished, he was very sympathetic toward her.

Thomas was a very kind-hearted, non-teasing, ten-year-old who loved animals, especially strays. He was also the only boy who looked like his father. He had brown hair with dark eyes. His brother, James, on the other hand, looked more like his mother and her side of the family. But he still had his father's twinkle in his eye. Thomas felt sorry that his dear sister had to give the kitten up, so he tried to comfort her. "Maybe you can get another cat sometime," he said reassuringly.

"Maybe," was all that Martha could muster because her eyes were brimming with tears again. She needed to regain her composure because there was a wagon coming around the bend and she did not want the driver seeing her in distress. But the smile she gave Thomas was all he needed.

What were Anna and Lydia doing back at home? They had been blowing up balloons for the party and had come into the living room to get more when Martha had been talking to Ashley.

They'd looked out the window to see Martha had given her kitten back to the obvious owner. They'd watched Martha slowly turn toward the door, and knew how heartbroken she was. Then both of them hurried upstairs to work on the balloons, and when Martha left, they got the whole story from Mom.

Feeling so sad for Martha, they set out to

make her feel better.

"What do you think we should do?" asked Anna.

"I don't know yet, but we need to figure up something really good," Lydia replied.

"I know! We could finish cleaning the yard for her. That's one of her chores to do for the party. I know that's not her favorite job to do. Why don't we do that?"

"That's a great idea, Anna!" exclaimed Lydia, her blue eyes twinkling, she jumped up and down, giving her brown hair a flounce, "let's go get the rake and clean up the old leaves from last winter."

"Yes! Then we'll get James and Dad to move the picnic tables under the old oak tree. Then we'll trim the grass and hedges. Then we'll probably need to work in the garden," said Anna.

"We need to get to work. I'll go get the rake while you start trimming the grass," Lydia offered.

"Okay, I can't wait to see the look on Martha's face when she sees this!" Anna beamed.

About an hour later Mom called Anna and Lydia to lunch and exclaimed, "Oh my, you girls have worked hard and Martha will be so surprised to see it!"

"We hope so," Lydia grinned.

"I know it. I just baked some fresh cookies if you want some after lunch."

"Oh, yes, thank you," said both girls smiling in unison.

They hurried inside and ate quickly then rushed back to finish their work while Mom laid Sarah and Elizabeth down for their afternoon nap.

The wagon was just nearing the driveway when Martha saw Anna and Lydia waiting. "Look at Lydia and Anna. I wonder what they are there for?"

As they got nearer, both girls started bouncing on their toes in excitement and when the wagon stopped, they exclaimed, "Wait till you see!"

"Wait till I see what?" asked Martha.

"It's a secret! But just wait till you see it."

"Oh, I see. It's a surprise," said Martha excitedly. "Well, why don't you two hop in the wagon with us and ride to the house and we'll see your secret?" Her two little sisters hopped in and started giggling lightly.

Once they were in front of the house, Martha gasped, "You cleaned the yard for me, and even got the picnic tables out under the big oak tree. Now I won't have to do it! How nice of you. Thank you SO much!" exclaimed Martha.

"We wanted to surprise you because you gave your kitten away," said Anna for both girls.

"Well, thank you both. You are such sweet and thoughtful sisters! Thomas, would you please unhitch the horses for me?"

"Sure, Martha, you go on inside and see Mom," replied Thomas with a broad smile.

"Thanks. Let's go," Martha put her arms around each sister's shoulder and they hurried inside as Lydia bubbled, "And Mommy made some cookies! The ones you really like. You know the big, chewy, chocolate chip cookies. I'm sure you could have some if you ask!"

Chapter 10
Preparing

It was a cool Monday morning and Martha and Anna were elbow high in flour making pastries for Saturday's upcoming party. Mom was working on her dress for the party; Sarah and Lydia were working in the garden and Elizabeth was in her highchair eating a cracker.

Suddenly the girls heard a knock at the door. "Anna, while I get that, could you fill these pies with these peaches I just cut up?" asked Martha, as she wiped her hands on her apron.

"Sure, Martha, but I wonder who that could be at this time of morning?" wondered Anna.

"Thanks. I'm wondering who it could be, too; perhaps the mailman with a package." Martha's eyes twinkled as she wiped her hands on her apron.

Martha hurried to the door and opened it to find her good friend, Polly, her older brother, Benjamin, and her younger sister, Selah.

"Oh, hello, it's so nice to see you. Come in. Is your mother with you?"

"No, she had to stay home but we wanted to come over and see if we could help with anything for the party on Saturday," announced Polly.

"Well, that's very kind of you. Please come and say hello to my Mom."

"We'd love to," Benjamin said.

After they said hello, Martha put them to work. "Polly, you can help Anna and me in the kitchen. Selah, you know where our garden is. Lydia and Sarah are in the garden now and I know they're probably in for some of your entertainment and your help. Benjamin, the boys are in the field. If you want to help, they'll probably be in for lunch in about an hour."

"Okay," the three eagerly agreed.

As Polly followed Martha happily into the kitchen, Benjamin went out to the fields and Selah went to the garden to help Sarah and Lydia.

Martha got an extra apron from the pantry for Polly and she put it on. Martha explained what she needed her to do. "Please start cutting up these apples and then sprinkle them with the lemon juice and cinnamon on the counter."

Polly nodded. "Okay, Martha."

They worked in silence for a few minutes until Polly spoke up, "May I ask what the order of the events will be?"

"Sure. Dad and Mom will renew their vows.

Then we'll eat, which is going to be simple, hamburgers and hot dogs, veggies, and for dessert, well—that's a surprise. But then Grandpa and Grandma will give a special speech to Mom and Dad. Don't tell. They don't know about it yet."

"Oh, don't worry. I can keep a secret," assured Polly.

"Then we will dance. I'm really excited about the dancing. I don't get many chances to do so. Does the plan please you?" asked Martha.

"Oh, yes, if only I could help you more. But I can only stay 'til this afternoon."

"Hey, I have an idea. Why don't you ask your parents and I'll ask mine, and if they both say yes, you can spend the night here before the party! You can help us make final preparations. You'll bring your party dress so we can prepare together, including Anna, Lydia, and Sarah, 'cause I'm in charge of their dresses and hair."

"That's a great idea!" exclaimed Polly and Anna at once. The three girls burst into giggles.

Chapter 11
FUN

The next morning, Martha woke up fresh and ready to start a new day. She and Anna dressed, washed up, did their hair, then went downstairs and out the back door to do their chores.

"Good morning, Thomas. Where's James?" Martha wondered as she approached Thomas who was milking the Knight's old brown cow, Cassie.

"He's still asleep. Mom thinks he may be having a growth spurt, so she wants him to have plenty of rest."

"Why don't I get a growth spurt?" asked Anna, curiously.

Martha and Thomas looked at each other, smiling, "You'll surely have a growth spurt soon," comforted Martha. Even though James and Anna were twins, they looked very different. James was sandy-haired and brown-eyed, while Anna was blonde-haired with blue eyes, and she was also shorter as well.

"Thomas, I'll help you since you have extra chores," offered Martha.

"That's very kind of you, Martha, but I think I can handle it. Dad says he wants to have a meeting after breakfast, so if you can hurry with your chores, perhaps you can persuade Mom to serve breakfast a little earlier.”

Martha put on her firmest expression. “Well, Thomas Peter Knight, for your information, I do not think I can...” she paused and Thomas held his breath hopefully. “...POSSIBLY resist this. You've gone and made me curious. Okay, I'll put on my sweetest smile and try to sweet talk Mom into serving breakfast earlier. I'll even offer to help her.”

“Thanks, Martha,” said Thomas.

Try as she might, Martha could not persuade her dear Mother to serve the morning meal any earlier. Poor girl, she was just about bursting with excitement.

Finally, it was time. After morning devotions and their monthly song being sung, Dad raised his hand for all the children to quiet down. “Okay everyone, I think everyone here knows that something is afoot. Well, your Mother and I have decided you children are being such good helpers and are working so hard...” he paused, extending their excitement, “...that we are going to go strawberry picking today. After we’re done picking strawberries, we’ll come back home and the girls will preserve half the berries, and the other half will be made into cakes and pies for the party. How does that sound?”

"That sounds like fun, Dad. When do we go?" asked Thomas.

"Right now," smiled Dad cheerfully. "Martha, I will put you in charge of getting the bonnets on every girl and getting them into the wagon which will pull up in front of the house in ten minutes. Boys, you help Mom with getting the baskets and I'll hitch up the wagon."

"Okay, Dad," said all the children in unison.

"Okay, children, here we are. Martha, you are in charge of Lydia and Sarah. Thomas and James, I want you to keep an eye out for Anna. Mom's going to carry Elizabeth in the sling. Lydia and Sarah, I want you to obey Martha now."

"Yes, Dad," replied both girls as Thomas and James assisted them to the ground.

As they all started out with baskets in hand, Martha and her sisters headed out in the lead and started picking strawberries.

"'Marta,'" started Sarah, "you taught me the Virginia Rrreel, the Patty Cake Polka, Windmills, and Carrrolina Prrromenade Are there any more I should learn?"

"Well, I looked at the list and there are about two more I need to teach you this afternoon, which are the Polka and the Waltz."

"Oh, that would be fun," said Sarah. "Let's hurry up and pick."

Once the family got back home, Martha put her apron on and washed her hands and started washing up the strawberries. She handed the sweet berries to Sarah who put them in the jar. Anna poured water into the full jars to keep the berries ripe and ready to eat for winter.

Once they had finished, about an hour later, Martha started making dough while Mom was working in the garden. Martha set Anna to work chopping up the strawberries and Sarah soaked them in a bowl of water.

Martha grabbed the flour, oil, a cup of water, and a rolling pin. She poured the flour into a bowl and added the oil and water, and added just a dab of honey to sweeten it up and started mixing.

Once it was halfway mixed, Martha added two eggs, but she thought that since she was doubling the recipe to double the eggs, so she pulled out the egg carton and opened it up. To her dismay, there were only three eggs. "Sarah, would you run out to the chicken coop and see if you can find two more eggs for me please?"

"Yes, Marta," said Sarah.

About five minutes later Sarah came in crying horribly and sobbed, "B-big Red scraped me!"

"Oh, that rooster, we really should get rid of him! I declare."

"O-oh, don't get rid of him," cried Sarah for she had inherited the same characteristic as Thomas and liked animals. She couldn't bear for Ol' Red to go away.

"Well, then, we'll just figure out something else then," Martha said to cheer her sister up. But inside she was boiling mad. She thought, *When will that rooster learn?!* Martha lifted Sarah into a chair and took a cool cloth and said, "This may sting a little. I'm sorry."

Indeed, it did sting and by the time Martha was done cleaning, Sarah was sobbing quietly. "I'm sorry that rooster did that to you. I think I hear Lydia in the living room. Why don't you go sit with her?"

"Okay," replied Sarah, gently getting off of the chair, "thank you."

Martha sighed; *I should have gone myself or at least sent Anna, who is older. How wrong of me. Jesus, forgive me. I was being lazy. I'll try harder.*

Later that night as Martha tucked Anna, Lydia, and Sarah in, and made sure Elizabeth was still sleeping soundly, she decided to write in her diary. She took it from the desk drawer along with a pen and started writing.

August 21st, 1930,

Dear God,

I had a big day! We went strawberry picking. We baked pies. My little sister, Sarah, got scraped by Ol' Red, our rooster, and we helped Dad sort out the tools in the barn. It was a good day. Last Sunday at church, Cathryn Williams was saying that there was to be a Christmas ball held the first Saturday in December. I hope I can go. I'm not sure if Dad will be able to take me, but hopefully either Thomas or James will. I guess we'll have to see.

Well, I better go now so as not to wake my sleeping sisters!

Your faithful servant,

Martha Rosemary Knight

Chapter 12
Finishing Up

Martha had just gotten back from fetching the mail when she noticed that there was a letter from Ashley, the girl who'd lost the kitten. Martha hurriedly opened the letter and read:

Dear Miss Martha,

Thank you for giving my kitten back to me. It was very kind and considerate of you.
I am taking good care of Liberty. Right now she is sitting by the window sunning.
Tell your sister, Lydia, that I would love to write her. I'll give my address at the bottom of the page.
THANK YOU AGAIN!

Your friend,

Ashley...

Martha closed the letter and put it in her apron pocket and got back to work wiping down the picnic tables. She thought: *I'm glad I gave Liberty back to Ashley. What if I hadn't? She would have been really sad.*

"Martha!" called Mom. "Would you come here, please?"

"Yes, Mom, I'm coming," called Martha. Martha came to her mother who was standing on the porch, "Mrs. Hard is sick and I need to go nurse her. I need you to watch the children. You can take a break now. The others are eating their lunch. The boys and Dad will head back out to the fields after lunch."

"Okay, Mom. After lunch I'll put Elizabeth and Sarah down for their nap and then Anna, Lydia, and I can clean the kitchen. Then we'll have a snack. Don't worry about us, but with the party so close are you sure you want to risk your health?"

"Martha, I appreciate your concern, but I care more about Mrs. Hard than a silly old party. Besides, Mrs. Hard has had a hard year, with her husband's death and her children living out east."

"I know, Mom. You are so considerate. I wish I could be as thoughtful as you. I really do hope Mrs. Hard gets better soon. I just can't help but be worried that you'll get sick and the party will be canceled."

"I know. I understand your feelings, but I put those feelings that I had away for a dear, dear friend."

"Okay, Mom. Don't worry about us. We'll be fine, and if you need me, just send for me."

"Alright, thank you, Martha. I know you'll take good care of our family. Anyway, if I'm not back by supper time, which I suspect, I won't be

back 'til tomorrow afternoon. There are beans in
the ice box and all you'll have to do is warm them
up. You could peel and cut up some potatoes to do
a potato casserole. We have a full loaf of bread, and
would you please make another loaf for me?"

"Sure, Mom, don't worry. You just take care of
Mrs. Hard," assured Martha.

Mom left about fifteen minutes later and
Martha went to the kitchen to eat her lunch.

"Marta, will we still have the party?" asked an
anxious Sarah.

"Sure we will," replied Martha, though she
wasn't completely sure there was going to be a
party. *Dear God, I really want there to be a party,
but if there's not, please help me to accept it.
Mom's right, a neighbor and friend is more
important than a party,* prayed Martha silently.

After lunch, Martha put Elizabeth and Sarah
down for their afternoon nap and then hurried
downstairs where Anna and Lydia were already
cleaning. Anna was mopping, and Lydia was
cleaning off the table.

Martha got the necessary things for making a
loaf of bread: flour, sugar, salt, yeast, and some
other ingredients and mixed them all together and
kneaded it and put it in a pan in a corner of the
counter to rise.

She thought she would go ahead and prepare supper when she looked at the clock and realized it was about time for her littlest sisters to get up from their nap.

She went upstairs to get them and took them downstairs and settled the three-and one-year-olds at the table for a little snack before supper time. "Martha, after Sarah finishes her snack, can we go out and play?" asked Lydia.

"That sounds fine with me. Please ask Anna to watch you, I need to work on supper."

"Yes, Martha, I'll be sure to ask her."

Martha started chopping up some potatoes that would go into a casserole. She could hear Anna, Lydia, and Sarah hustling to finish their snack so that they could play outside.

"Don't gorge your snack down. You've got plenty of time," reprimanded their oldest sister.

They slowed down, and about five minutes later she heard their chairs scrape on the wood floor as they took care of their trash and headed outside. "Bye, Martha!" called Lydia.

"Bye, be careful!"

"We will."

Martha worked diligently on supper preparations, glancing out towards her siblings playing with Nellie, their Great Pyrenees. She had just placed the potato casserole in the oven when she heard a loud scream. Martha broke into a run out the back door and what met her sight was Vernon on his hind legs, whinnying. "NO! Girls, get back!"

Anna, Lydia, and Sarah were clinging to one another, scared to death of the rearing horse five feet away. Anna looked at Martha and suddenly regained her senses and urged the girls to run to the house. Martha looked at the powerful horse; he was three or four times her size and he wouldn't stop neighing. She could tell he was terrified.

"Girls!" yelled Martha to her sisters who were now at the safety of the porch, "I'm going to get dad and the boys. You stay right there, don't move from the house!"

Anna nodded and drew her two sisters closer.

Martha ran her hardest to the fields where her father and brothers were working. "Dad! Dad! Vernon is going crazy in the barnyard, I need your help!"

Dad looked up, questioningly, for he hadn't heard what she had said as she was farther away. She repeated what she was saying and when he understood, he bolted to where she was motioning.

Martha held her breath nervously as Vernon reared up again in front of her dad, "James, get me the gun from the house," said Dad, yelling.

"Thomas, get me a rope from the barn!"

Both boys sprinted to do as they were told. They arrived back at their father at the same time. Dad widened the loop hole that was already in the rope, and started swinging. He swung and he was blessed that it fit around the wild horse's neck the first time. He took a step towards Vernon, all the while talking soothingly. Once he had the horse under control, he had Thomas hold the rope while he took the gun from James and shot a rattlesnake that was slithering away.

Once he buried the snake, he brushed a hand across his forehead and breathed a sigh of relief. "Is everyone alright?" he asked, looking at each of his children in turn.

Everyone affirmed that they were okay, that they just had had a bad scare.

Dad felt a shiver go down his spine as he thought about what might have happened. Vernon could have gotten bit and had to be shot, and even worse, what happened if any of his children had gotten bit by the rattler or trampled by the horse? "Everyone, I think we should pray and thank God that nobody got hurt."

They all gathered in a circle and Dad prayed, "Lord Jesus, we thank You and praise You for Your amazing, timely, and perfect protection of not only my children, but also Vernon. Please keep the snakes away so they will not bother us anymore. Thank you, Lord. In Your Name we pray, amen."

"Martha," said Dad, turning to his eldest daughter, "the boys and I are going to finish up in the fields, but we'll be back shortly. Girls, you can continue playing. Don't let this incident make you scared. Vernon is secure in his stall now and I and the boys will make certain endeavors that it will not happen again."

"Yes sir," everyone replied.

As Dad and the boys headed back out to the fields, Lydia turned to Martha and said, "Martha, I'm scared. I don't want to play outside here again without Daddy watching us."

"Lydia, remember what Daddy said? He said not to worry. You're perfectly safe, and I'll be out here as soon as the casserole is done in the oven, which will be soon. And Anna will be outside with you."

"Okay, Martha. Come on, Sarah and Anna, let's go!"

The girls continued playing outside until supper time and then everyone gathered around the table and once again gave thanks for the protection they had had that afternoon.

Chapter 13
Helping Others

"Okay, everyone, it's time to head on over to Mrs. Hard's to get Mom and help clean and weed Mrs. Hard's house and garden," said Dad on Friday morning.

Martha was going to bake fresh bread and cookies and make a fresh casserole for when Mrs. Hard was well enough to feel like eating. Lydia and Sarah were going to weed the garden. Anna was going to clean the living room and the parlor, while the boys were going to give Mrs. Hard's pair of matched gray horses exercise, milk the cows and feed the chickens.

"Martha, do you have the picnic lunch?" asked Dad.

"Yes, Dad, but please don't ask what it is. It's a surprise," replied Martha with a smile. James eyed the basket and licked his lips.

"Okay, Martha, I won't ask. Would you make sure Elizabeth has some diapers in a bag?"

"Yes, sir," and Martha turned to make sure.

When they were in the wagon heading toward their neighbor's, James asked, "Oh, please, Martha, give me a hint."

"What hint?" asked Martha mischievously.

"You know what I'm talking about."

"I do?" asked Martha, pretending not to know. She loved to joke around with her brother sometimes.

"Martha Rosemary Knight, you know very well what I'm talking about. Just one little hint, PLEASE?"

"Well, I guess I might know what you're talking about, and NO! I will not give you one little hint. It's a surprise and you're just going to have to wait," replied Martha playfully.

"Well, I may just have to sneak a peek in that basket of yours then."

"You better not!" said Martha poking him gently in the ribs.

"OW!" exclaimed James acting like he was hurt.

Then suddenly, Dad turned around and eyed Martha carefully, "Is everything okay back there?"

"Oh, Martha just poked me, Dad," moaned James playfully.

"Okay, Martha, start acting more lady-like,"

Dad pretended to frown.

Martha knew he was joking but still she blushed when he playfully rebuked her.

"And James, be a man," Dad tried to look stern and hold in his laughter, but his loud booming laugh soon had the whole family laughing away.

Once they got to Mrs. Hard's house, they all crowded into the elderly lady's room where she was sitting in her arm chair.

Then Martha got to work in the kitchen starting with making two loaves of bread. After she got that done she started making the casserole. When she almost got to the end of making the Knights' favorite potato casserole, she couldn't remember right off how much cheese she was supposed to put in and on top of it. She went upstairs and knocked on the door of the room her mother was in. When her Mom answered it, Martha hurriedly asked her how much to put in. When she got her answer she went back to the kitchen and finished up the cooking. After she finished, she decided to go and set the picnic.

She'd made cucumber sandwiches, peanut butter and jam sandwiches, brownies, and two thermoses of lemonade.

Then suddenly James popped out from

behind a tree and with Thomas in tow.

"You are a very persistent young man," said Martha.

"I know, but I wanna know what you have for lunch," said James, eyeing the delicious food,

"Hmm, cucumber, my personal favorite." He snatched up one before Martha could catch him.

"Sandwich stealer," said Martha. And before she could do anything, Thomas snatched one too.

"Thomas and James, make yourselves useful. Go and tell everyone that lunch is ready. Now— scoot."

After lunch, Martha cleaned up the mess and was about to help in the garden when Anna came rushing out onto the porch. "Martha, something smells like it's burning!"

"Oh no!" cried Martha, "the casserole!"

The two girls rushed into the house and Martha put the oven mitts on, opened the oven door, and pulled out a burned potato casserole. Martha groaned. What had she done to the casserole?

"Perhaps the cheese is the only thing burned Martha," offered Anna.

"That's a good idea. I'll check." Martha pulled out a spatula and carefully and delicately pulled the charred cheese upwards. She figured out that the cheese was the only thing burned; the potatoes and cheese mixture were unharmed by the overcooking. Martha breathed a sigh of relief, and then asked Anna to fetch the block of mozzarella cheese and to grate some of it down. She would just sprinkle new cheese on the hot chunks of potatoes and it would slowly melt. She was going to dispose of the burned cheese. As she did so, she opened the kitchen windows to allow fresh air in so it wouldn't smell so much like smoke.

Fifteen minutes later, the job was done and both girls went back to what they were doing. "Thank you for helping me, Anna."

"You're welcome," replied the eight-year-old cheerfully.

She helped water the plants and then decided to make some lemonade.

She cut some lemons in half and squeezed them, using her fingers to keep the seeds from falling in. Then she put some water in and sprinkled sugar to sweeten it. She put the cups on a tray and served Lydia and Sarah, then she went out to the barn where Dad was finishing milking the cows and the boys were raking the loft and stalls.

"Ah, thanks, Martha," exclaimed Dad

gratefully.

Then James and Thomas came down from the loft and grabbed their cups. "Thanks, Martha," Thomas smiled.

"A lemon of a toast to Martha," said James jokingly.

"Okay you two, get back to work," groaned Martha.

Martha took a cup to Anna who was cleaning the parlor and getting ready to move on to the living room.

"The parlor looks great, Anna. You've done a great job with it," exclaimed Martha encouragingly.

"Thanks for the drink, too," replied Anna.

Next, Martha headed upstairs where Mom was nursing a sleeping Mrs. Hard and where Elizabeth was taking her nap in the corner of the room on a cot.

"Mom, I'll take a turn nursing while you go downstairs and have a break if you like. I have some cool lemonade on the kitchen table."

"You know, Martha, a half-hour break from in here would be nice."
"Well, I'll just sit in here while you go take a

break. When is Ms. Flowers coming?"

"She should be here at two o'clock, which is in about an hour. If you could take over for about a half hour, I'll watch for the rest, while you get the girls ready to go. You've been such a help. Thank you."

Martha bathed Mrs. Hard's neck and forehead with cool water. About fifteen minutes later Mrs. Hard woke up and yawned.

"Oh, Miss Martha Knight," she said pleasantly, "what a nice surprise. I really am thankful that you and your family are helping me out. I'm just sad that I can't come to your party."

"It's our pleasure to help a kind friend. If I remember correctly, it was you who brought a meal to us about year and a half ago when Elizabeth was born."

"Well, that is what neighbors do. Would you please read to me from my Bible? It always helps me when I'm feeling sick and peevish."

"Sure, how about a Psalm?" suggested Martha.

"Perfect, how about Psalm 15?" asked Mrs. Hard.

"Okay then, Psalm 15," replied Martha. Mrs.

Hard drifted off to a peaceful sleep to the sound of Martha's gentle reading.

It was about six o'clock when there was a knock on the door. Martha put down the hymnals she was carrying and went to the door and opened it. It was Polly and her Father.

"Hello, won't you come in?" Martha could barely contain her excitement.

"Yes, thank you Miss Knight," said Mr. McShire, tipping his hat playfully.

Polly and her Father came in and George started talking with Dad while Martha led Polly upstairs to put away her suitcase.

"I want to show you my dress," said Polly opening her suitcase and taking her new party dress out and laying it on the bed.

"Oh, Polly, it's beautiful!" exclaimed Martha. "You must have worked hard on it."

"Yes, Mother helped me with the collar," replied Polly.

Polly's dress was a pretty periwinkle color, with lace at the collar and at the bottom of the skirt.

"Let me show you my dress," said Martha excitedly. But just then, Dad called the girls down for devotions.

"Well, I'll show you after," said Martha. "Come on, let's go down for devotions. I'm so glad you are able to be here and I really appreciate your help on finishing up my dress."

"It's my pleasure, Martha."

George McShire had accepted the invitation to stay for Bible study and was seated in Mom's rocking chair, Dad and Mom were on the couch, Martha and Polly were in the chairs and the others were sitting at Dad's feet.

"Today, we are going to read Philippians 2:3. James would you read that to us, please?"

"Yes, Dad," replied James. "'Philippians 2:3. *'Let nothing be done through strife or vainglory; but in lowliness of mind let each esteem other better than themselves.'* What does that mean, Dad? I'm a bit confused. Does it mean I need to give up my play things every time someone else wants it?" asked James.

"Well, not exactly. Not that you should not be a gentleman and share your toys. Here's an example. If you were to meet a stranger on the street who said he was better at baseball than you, your first reaction would be to talk back and say that you were better. I think what this is saying is that you would put your pride away and say, 'All right, you are better than me,' to make him feel good."

"Oh, that sounds hard to do," said James seriously.

"It takes patience and practice to learn, but if we try hard enough and ask God to help us, I'm certain we can do it," said Dad. "Okay, everybody, let's sing a hymn. How about *For the Beauty of the Earth*?

Everybody started singing, young and old, just singing the first verse:
For the beauty of the earth,
For the glory of the skies,
For the love which from our birth
Over and around us lies,
Lord of all, to Thee we raise
This our hymn of grateful praise.

After devotions and evening play time were finished, Polly and Martha went to tuck Sarah, Lydia, and Elizabeth down in their beds and then Martha lit a lamp and set it on a side table. She went to her wardrobe in her room and pulled out a pretty very light daffodil-colored dress that had ruffles at the bottom.

"Oh, Martha, it's beautiful! You will look like a princess!" Polly gushed.

Martha grinned. "My Mom's dress is a

surprise; only my parents know what it looks like. Mom has given us a few hints but they haven't helped any," said Martha in a whisper. "Well, I suppose we ought to get to work on the dress and then head to bed. We have a big day tomorrow. Why don't we go down to the kitchen and work? We'd have more room."

They worked the next half-hour on Martha's dress and then they put their nightgowns on, brushed their teeth, undid their hair, and brushed it. Then they hopped into bed, which was really full with three girls in it. Martha, Polly, and Anna wiggled and giggled for a few minutes, then talked quietly for about half an hour before going to sleep.

Chapter 14
The Big Day

Martha woke to the feeling that someone was shaking her. She opened up her eyes and saw Sarah, who was nearly jumping with excitement.

"Today is the party!" exclaimed Sarah.

"Yes, it is. Now let me get you dressed into your day dress."

Martha carefully and quietly stepped onto the floor and slipped Sarah's night gown off and pulled a nice dark blue dress on her and buttoned it and put on an apron. Then she said to her, "I need you to wash your face while I get dressed so I can put your hair in curlers for the party."

"Yes, 'Marta,'" replied Sarah.

While Martha dressed, Sarah cleaned her face and brushed her hair and then waited quietly for Martha to finish dressing.

Then about two minutes later Martha came out from behind the curtain her Mom put up for privacy in the corner. "Okay, I need you to stand very still while I put your hair in curlers, okay?"

"Yes, 'Marta,'" Sarah assented obediently.

Just when Martha was finished with Sarah's

hair, Polly woke up.

"You should have wakened me," said Polly.

"Nonsense; we have a big day ahead and you need your beauty sleep, me lady," said Martha playfully.

"No more sleep than you need," replied Polly rubbing her sleepy eyes.

"Well, if you'll help me curl Anna's and Lydia's hair we can go down to breakfast. Mother said last night that the boys would do us girls' chores."

"Oh good," said Polly, waking Anna and starting her hair while Martha did Lydia's. When Polly was done curling Anna's hair, she hurried to dress.

"Let's pray," said Dad at the end of morning devotions.

"Dear Jesus, Thank You for this beautiful day You have blessed us with. Lord, we have a busy day ahead of us and also a fun one. We ask that You place guardian angels around us and our friends today as they come to the party then back to their homes. Please bless them for their kindness in attending our occasion. And we also thank You for allowing us another pair of hands to help us. Please bless her and her family. We pray this in Your most

Holy Name. Amen."

"Here's what I need from everyone. Polly and Martha will be in charge of laying the tablecloths and the name tags. Thomas and James, I want you to carry out the benches to the yard to the left of the oak tree about fifteen feet from where the picnic tables are. Anna, Lydia, and Sarah, I want you to help your Mother. Anna, you're in charge of Elizabeth at least 'til after lunch."

"Yes sir," said the children in unison.

About ten minutes later, Polly and Martha where getting the tablecloths from the shelves and the name placements and carried them out and started putting them on.

"I don't know yet what I'm going to do with my hair for the party," sighed Martha, frustrated.

"Why don't we try a different style?" suggested Polly.

"My parents are awfully strict about what I do to my hair."

Polly assured, "I have the perfect hair style for you, and it's not too vain."

"Really?"

"Oh, I'm positive. I'll describe it to your

parents at lunch time."

The girls finished up and headed back into the house to help Mom and the other girls 'til lunch time.

"Your parents said yes! It sounds fine!" said Polly excitedly.

"Oh goodie," smiled Martha. "But first we need to get some blankets because we won't have enough picnic tables. At two o'clock, we can go upstairs. The guests are supposed to start arriving at 4:00. So that will give us an hour and a half to prepare."

The girls headed out with stacks of blankets when they heard something strange. "I wonder what that could be?" inquired Martha.

"I don't know," Polly replied.

"It sounds like it came from the barn. Let's go," said Martha. She and Polly hurried toward the sound and found poor Nellie with her leg in a trap.

"Who would do this?" cried Martha. "My Dad puts traps in the woods. This one is a bear trap and there is rarely a bear in this neck of the woods. This trap was put here deliberately. Polly, would you please go and get my Dad? He should be in the barn. Tell him what happened and hurry, please."
Polly ran to the barn. When she found Dad

she cried, "Mr. Knight, N-Nellie is badly hurt. Her leg is caught in a b-bear t-trap."

"Okay, let me gather up a few tools. Everything is going to be all right," Dad told her, gathering up the necessary tools. He and Polly quickly headed toward Martha and Nellie.

"Is she going to be okay, Dad?" asked Martha worriedly.

"Yes, I think so, as long as we can keep infection from setting in. Would you hand me that gauze and the antiseptic, please?"

Martha handed him what he needed and then went back to rocking back and forth on her heels. For all of Nellie's mischief, she was loved deeply and Martha wasn't sure how she would handle it if Nellie did die or lose her leg.

"Martha, I know you're upset, but you still have a wedding to be in. It's just about two o'clock. Why don't you and Polly head upstairs and start preparing for the party? I promise Nellie will be taken care of."

"Yes sir." She knew if she didn't, she would get a lecture about not worrying from her Dad.

Both the girls headed somberly up the stairs and into the girls' room. While Polly heated an iron to curl part of Martha's hair, Martha washed her face and hands, combed out her hair and tried to calm herself.

"Martha, your Father's right. It would be a shame for you to be all down in the dumps for the party. And plus, no young man wants to dance with a young lady who's all blue in the spirit," Polly said teasingly.

"You're right. You're a good friend, Polly. Now what are you going to do to my hair? I hope it's not a plan to whack off my whole head," Martha lifted a mischievous brow.

"Oh, no, I'm not that disastrous," said Polly, mocking being hurt.

"Well then, I guess I just have to trust you with my hair. When you're done with it, I'll do yours."

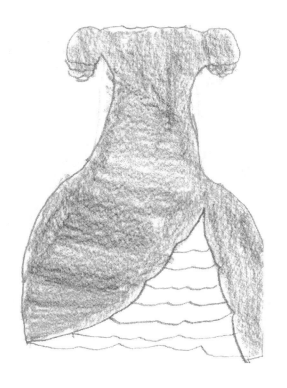

Chapter 15
Continued...

"Oh, doesn't this look yummy?" asked Martha, as she placed another casserole that her mother made into the oven.

"Yes, it does," replied Polly.

"I sure hope Nellie will be okay," said Martha.

"I hope so too, but we shouldn't spend the whole wedding worrying about her. Your Dad said that she should be fine."

"I know. I'll try not to worry," Martha promised. "Anyway, the guests should start arriving any moment. You know, I'm reminded of a verse in Philippians that states: *'Don't worry about anything, but in everything, through prayer and petition with thanksgiving, let your requests be made known to God.'*"

"You're right, Martha, come on," replied Polly, starting outside.

As if to answer her, a wagon started coming up the drive and Thomas, who was in charge of tying their horses to the hitching post, greeted them and sent them to their seats where Martha waited to hand out programs.

Martha sighed happily. "Well, since our first

guests have arrived, I suppose I need to go hand
out the programs."

"All right, I'll see if any of your sisters need
their bows retied," Polly offered.

"Good. I can't tell you how much you've
helped out today," Martha said appreciatively.

"Well, I had a lot of fun!" Polly told her.
Martha went to greet their first guests, Doctor
Barns and his wife, Angela.

"Hello there. How are you today?" greeted
Martha.

"We are doing marvelous on this special
occasion," replied Dr. Barns.

"You look very pretty, Martha." Mrs. Barns
beamed.

"Thank you. Please hand the reins to Thomas.
Here are some programs I made, and you may sit
here." Martha held her hand toward two chairs.

"Thank you," said Mrs. Barns, while Dr. Barns
handed the reins to Thomas.

"Oh, I think I see the Poltors arriving, and
look—that must be Miss Under. Oh, I can't wait to
meet her!"

About thirty minutes later, Pastor Share stood on the platform that James and Dad had built together and opened the ceremony in prayer.

"Dear Heavenly Father, as we gather together at our dear friends' house, let us be considerate of others and let Mr. and Mrs. Knight always cherish each other for the rest of their lives. Amen."

Then as if from nowhere, Dad appeared in a jet black suit. Anna, Lydia, and Sarah followed as flower girls and Martha as a junior bridesmaid. Then Mom's maid of honor, also her sister-in-law, Caitlyn, fondly known as Catie, came slowly down the aisle. She'd come with Grandma and Grandpa Knight and they were staying in the Knight's guest house for a whole week. She was Dad's sister.

Finally Mom appeared holding a bunch of white roses. She was wearing a pure white dress with a veil over her face and a bustle in the back. The lovely "bride" walked slowly up the aisle.

Martha could see her smile, a girlish smile that seemed to take her breath away. Her mother was beautiful! It was almost as if she were taken back in time to when her Mother and Father were first being wed. And Father—Martha could see the pride in his eyes that this was his beloved, his beautiful bride.

Once Mom got to the altar, Dad lifted the veil and revealed his bride's face and took her hands in his and turned toward the Pastor.

"Peter Benjamin Knight," began the pastor, "you took Rosemary as your lawfully wedded wife, to love and cherish all the days of your life. Do you repent of your promise?"

"Not for a minute or second," replied Peter with love in his eyes.

"Rosemary Jane Knight," said the pastor, turning to the beaming Mrs. Knight, "you took Peter as your lawfully wedded husband, to love and cherish all the days of your life. Do you repent of your promise?"

"Peter, I said this when we were first wed. *'For wherever you go, I will go, and wherever you live, I will live; your people will be my people, and your God will be my God. Where you die, I will die and there I will be buried. May the LORD do this to me, and even more, if anything but death separates you and me.'* [Ruth 1:16-17] So, no, I have not even thought about breaking my promise."

"Peter and Rosemary, in so much as the two of you have agreed to live together in holy matrimony, I now joyously declare you again to be a faithful husband and wife. Whom God hath joined together, let no one put asunder. You may kiss the bride."

"You were wonderful, Martha!" exclaimed Rose Williams.

"Thank you," Martha smiled back, giving her friend a hug. "Do you want to come with me? I think Pastor Share is going to say the blessing over the food."

"Sure, but first let's go find Cathryn. She'll want to come too," suggested Rose.

They found Cathryn talking to Polly and Jane Kate. When they saw Rose and Martha they hurried over and surrounded Martha with giggles and little hugs.

"Can you imagine we'll be walking down the aisle when we are of age?" asked Jane excitedly.

"I know. I was thinking about when my parents were first wed. When I looked into their eyes, it was as if they were taken back." Martha shook the dreams from her head. "We came to see if you wanted to eat with us. I think Pastor Share is going to say the blessing over the food soon."

"Yes, we'd love to join you!" exclaimed Cathryn.

The girls walked over, talking about the dance later that night.

After the blessing was said all the guests went

first to get their food and when Martha finally got to eat, she was utterly starved. Cathryn, Rose, and Polly had waited to eat with Martha and were starving too.

"So, Martha, what dances are we going to do?" asked an excited Jane.

"Well, first will be the waltz, which my parents will start, and then the Virginia Reel, then the Polka, the Sweet Hearts Promenade, and a few others," replied Martha.

As everyone finished their meal, an elderly couple stood on the stage and the elder Mr. Knight cleared his throat. Everyone became quiet and turned their attention to Gregory Knight. "Peter and Rosemary Knight, when I attended your wedding eighteen years ago, I knew that our precious Lord and Savior, Jesus Christ, was the foundation for your marriage. You both have treated each other with the utmost respect, honor, and love. You have kept this bond of marriage sacred, and for that, I'm proud to call you both my son and daughter-in-law." There was a catch in Gregory's voice, but he regained his composure and continued, "Peter, you are a fine man of God and you have been a dutiful and loving husband. Rosemary, when I saw you, I knew that you were the perfect wife for my son. As you continue on this path of marriage, I encourage you to keep on showing love and compassion for each other, for when your marriage is strong; you're setting a good example for your children…"

After the speech was finished, Dad gave the signal for Mrs. Williams, with Martha's help, to bring out the dessert. Dad put an arm around his wife, who was dabbing at her eyes with a handkerchief

As Nancy Williams and Martha slowly came out with the surprise dessert, everyone turned their eyes upon them. Setting the delicate treat on the table, Mrs. Williams took the cover off and revealed a beautiful cake. It was a huge white layered cake with red roses intricately designed on it. In bold letters, it read: CONGRATULATIONS ON 18 YEARS OF MARRIAGE!

"Okay everyone," said Gregory, who was still on the stand. "Mrs. Leslie McShire, Mrs. Nancy Williams, and Mrs. Janelle Share have graciously volunteered to distribute the cake. If you would like some, please line up horizontally at the table…"

A bit later, after Martha and her friends were done eating, Pastor Share clapped his hands for attention. "Okay, everyone," he announced. "Let the dancing begin! Peter, Rosemary, come on out here!"

As Dad and Mom started dancing, Thomas came up behind Martha and asked, "May I have this dance, dear sister?"

"Yes you may, kind sir," she replied with exaggerated politeness and a silly smile.

As her brother led her out on the dance floor, the other girls arrived. Samuel Poltor danced the waltz with his future bride. Cathryn danced with Fred Gates. Jane danced with her older brother, Harry, and Polly danced with her brother, Benjamin.

Half way through the waltz, Dad turned to everybody and said in a loud voice, "How about a tap waltz, folks?"

A round of excited yeses filled the lawn. So the music began and off they went, with Martha starting off with Thomas.

About a minute later Harry Gates walked up and patted Thomas on the shoulder. "Why don't you let me dance with your beautiful sister?"

"You may be doing me a favor, Harry. My feet are about ready to fall off," laughed Thomas.

Harry took a turn with Martha, and about two minutes later, Fred Kate came up and stole Martha from him. And on and on it went....

Chapter 16
A Wonderful Summer

The next morning, Martha came into the kitchen from doing her morning chores and stood beside her mom who was making eggs.

"Mom, did you have fun last night?" asked Martha.

"Yes, I did," replied Mom.

"Dad was so handsome and you looked very beautiful. I'm glad Grandma, Grandpa, and Aunt Catie were able to come," smiled Martha, giving her mother a hug.

"I'm glad they were able to come, too, dear. You looked very beautiful yourself."

"I had a lot of fun."

"It was a nice time for all. Martha, will you please set the table? I know that it is usually Anna's and Lydia's job but I decided to let them sleep in just this morning."

"Yes ma'am." Martha took some plates from the shelf.

"Okay, everyone," started Dad after morning devotions, "Today we undertake the task of cleaning up. Martha, I want you to take the table cloths and pick up the blankets. Thomas and James, I want you to put the benches back where they belong. I need to go to the fields today, and after lunch, Thomas and James, you'll come too. Anna, you're in charge of Elizabeth and Sarah. Lydia, you help Grandma and Mom in any way you can. Okay everybody, hop to it." Just then there was a knock at the door. Grandpa got up and answered it.

"Oh, hello Aaron and Nancy, come in."

The Williams family stepped through the door and Aaron spoke. "I thought you could use some help today."

"We sure could. Thank you."

"Well, then set us to work," said Aaron.

"Okay," began Dad looking gratefully at their kind friends. "Cathryn, would you please help Martha this morning?"

"Yes, sir," Cathryn agreed with excitement.

"Rose," smiled Mr. Knight to the younger sister, "would you please help Anna with the younger children?"

"Yes, sir," replied Rose.

"And Timothy, you can help James and Thomas. Aaron, why don't you come and help me in the fields? Nancy, I'm sure that my mom and wife could use your help; thank you all again for coming."

So everybody got to work.

"Whoo! This is hard work!" said Martha as she continued working with Cathryn. "Thank you for helping, Cathryn."

"You're very welcome. I'm glad that we were able to help." Cathryn folded a blanket and placed it on the growing pile.

"Martha, Cathryn!" called Lillian Knight. "Come and help set out lunch for the men, please."

"Yes, Grandma, we're coming!" replied Martha. "Come on. Let's hurry and wash up and help Mom and Grandma. I think we are having peanut butter and jelly sandwiches and cucumber sandwiches, and for dessert there's apple pie."

"Yum, that sounds so good after all that work," said Cathryn.

"Thank you so much for helping us. It has made the day go faster."

"Oh, glad we could help. But we better hurry. If I'm not mistaken, there are the men coming now."

"Then we do need to hurry," replied Martha. As the two girls broke into a run, Peter and Aaron Williams were having a conversation.

"So you say that your dog, Nellie, got her leg in a bear trap?" asked Mr. Williams.

"Yes, Aaron, and I don't think it was an accident."

"How come?"

"The trap was laid right behind the barn and I asked the boys about it and they said they didn't put it there. And I know that I didn't. Something's fishy around here."

Aaron nodded, "Yes, and a little creepy, too."

"Yes, it is. I'm just going to keep a close eye out on the farm."

"Yes, I would too," replied Aaron.

After lunch Cathryn and Martha laid Elizabeth and Sarah, as well as Jimmie and Kathy Williams, down for their afternoon naps. Then they went to the pantry where Nellie laid on a mat with her leg wrapped up. Martha gently unwrapped the cloth and put on more antiseptic and put gauze over that and wrapped it with cloths again. Then the two just sat there meditating, friend with friend.

"I'm going to find out who did this," Martha promised quietly.

"Martha, do you really think this is your business? Why not just leave it to your Dad?" Cathryn's eyes were filled with worry for her friend.

"Maybe you're right, but I want to know who did this," replied Martha with a bit of bitterness.

"Well, the school year is getting ready to start next week and you may not have enough time to think about that," said Cathryn.

"I'm so glad our parents homeschool us," exclaimed Martha.

"Me too, they saved us the long one mile walk, too," giggled Cathryn.

"Yes, I feel kind of sorry for the other children," said Martha.

And the girls went into another round of giggles.

Chapter 17
God's Servant

"Ah, that feels so good," exclaimed Martha. She had just put her feet in the cool water of the stream. She leaned back against a tree and sighed, "What an interesting Summer I've had. We found out we were going to have a party. Samuel Poltor is getting married this coming January. Irene Williams came for a visit from Colorado, and we are going to write to each other. Then there is the Depression everyone's talking about. I wonder how it's going to affect us? I found a kitten and I named her 'Jubilee' until I gave her back to her original owner; she was so happy. I did the right thing." Then there was that wild buggy ride that sent another shudder through her spine. What if Samuel Poltor had not come along? Where would she and her sister be right now? "Thank You, God, for protecting us." She thanked her Savior again. Anna became a Christian and there certainly had been a dramatic change in her young sister. She was more patient and slow to anger. She had more self-control when something happened. There was a true change in Anna. Then there was James' new fishing pole that Martha bought him because his old one had gotten lost in the pond and it was all her fault. Martha smiled at how her dear brother was so excited about his new pole. Then came the party, oh how grand it was! She also had fun while helping Mrs. Hard when she was sick. Yes, it had been a good summer, a long one, but a good one.

"Thank You, God, for all Your blessings!"

About an hour later, Martha headed back toward the house and started to help her mom with supper. They'd planned a meal of hamburgers and fried potatoes, tossed salad, and for dessert, strawberry pie.

She went to get a jar of the delicious red berries and whipped up a light whipped cream to go on top. She also put together a little sauce to mix in with the strawberries. When she was finished, she placed the pie into the ice box to cool before dessert.

Next she started on the salad, chopping up cucumbers from their plentiful garden, also cutting up tomatoes and strawberries from their recent picking. She pulled a head of lettuce from the ice box and started putting leaves of lettuce into the bowl of fruits and vegetables and mixed that all together. Then she made a loaf of bread. Then she took over the churning of the butter.

"Wow, Mom, I didn't know you did so much work. I'm all tuckered out!" exclaimed Martha after evening devotions. Dad and Thomas were playing checkers. James was reading a book. Anna and Lydia were playing cat's cradle. Sarah was looking at a picture book and Mom and Martha were working on a new quilt.

"Thank you, honey, for saying that. I do try

hard to make everybody happy, but I know that's not always possible in this life."

"I know, and I want you to know that I acknowledged all that you really do today."

Mom blushed prettily and said, "It is just what needs to be done. You'll be a mother someday and you will work as hard as I do."

"Thank you, Mom. I'm trying hard to be like you."

"I know you are, darling. Let's be done with the quilting for tonight. I need to put Elizabeth down for bed."

"Okay, Mom. I want to check on Nellie one more time before I head to bed."

"Okay, dear," replied Mom.

After Martha checked on Nellie she trudged up the stairs and opened the door, lit a lamp, sat down, took her diary out and started writing:

August 28th 1930

Dear God,

Thank You for blessing me with so many things. You've blessed me with a loving family, friends, a good church, our dog, Nellie. Please

God, make her better, please! I wonder who would do such a thing? I want to find out. But as we are getting ready to start a new school year, please let me have a good attitude and self-control for the adventure ahead. I wonder what will be around the next corner? How will the Stock Market Crash affect us?

But I know that whatever happens You will be with my family and me.

Love, Your servant and princess forever! Martha Rosemary Knight

Martha put her diary away and took out her Bible and opened it up to Ecclesiastes 3:1-8 and read

"To every thing there is a season,

and a time to every purpose under the heaven:

A time to be born, and a time to die;

A time to plant, and a time to pluck up that which is planted;

A time to kill, and a time to heal;

a time to break down, and a time to build up;

A time to weep, and a time to laugh;

a time to mourn, and a time to dance;

A time to cast away stones, and a time to gather stones together;

a time to embrace, and a time to refrain from embracing;

A time to get, and a time to lose;

a time to keep, and a time to cast away;

A time to rend, and a time to sew;

A time to keep silence, and a time to speak;

A time to love, and a time to hate;

A time of war, and a time of peace."

Martha thought for a minute more. *There IS a time for everything; that is so amazing. The way You plan things is just wonderful, Lord. I can't wait to find out the next adventure You have planned for me.* When she was finally ready, Martha said her prayers, closed her Bible and snuggled under the covers in her warm bed into sweet dreams.

~*~*~*~*~*~*~*~*~*~*~*~*~*~*~*~*~*~*~*
~*~*~*

I hope you enjoyed meeting Martha and her family! Wonder what will happen next in Martha's life, and what new adventures she will have? Find out in

Book Two
<u>Martha's Mysterious Stranger</u>
by Bekah O'Brien

91352739R00076

Made in the USA
Columbia, SC
20 March 2018